A sexy female voice singsonged, "Hello, gorgeous."

James grinned in the darkness of his bedroom. Yep. It was definitely the blonde who'd flirted with him earlier. Her body made contact with the mattress and he sensed rather than saw that she was naked.

"Why don't you switch on the light?" He'd love to get a look at her.

"I like the dark," she whispered. "And it's *very* dark in here." When her voice hitched in excitement, it seemed clear that having sex with him was high on her list of priorities. There was nothing that James loved more than being on a woman's "to-do" list.

But he was a gentleman at heart. "Are you sure you know what you're doing here?"

She laughed. "Oh, you want me to consent." She leaned over, her scent engulfing him. "I do, gorgeous."

For a second everything went silent. Yes, this cinched it. Sex was on her agenda. Heat pooled in James's belly and teased his groin. When he'd gotten into bed tonight, getting lucky had been the last thing on his mind....

He tossed back the covers, feeling a sleepy stir of air hit his naked body. "Abracadabra," he said. "C'mon in...."

Dear Reader,

There's nothing funnier or sexier to me than the idea of finding a stranger in your bed...especially a gorgeous hunk of a man you've never seen before, with whom you've shared the best passion of your life!

I hope you'll enjoy this addition to Temptation's great WRONG BED series. When a woman casts a spell for a night of hot, sizzling sex, she gets everything a woman might want in such a bed partner—except it's the wrong bed and the wrong guy. Or is he?

I had loads of fun with this one, so I hope you will, too!

Very best,

Jule McBride

Books by Jule McBride

HARLEQUIN TEMPTATION
866—NAUGHTY BY NATURE
875—THE HOTSHOT*
883—THE SEDUCER*
891—THE PROTECTOR*

*Big Apple Bachelors

HARLEQUIN BLAZE
67—THE SEX FILES
91—ALL TUCKED IN...

Don't miss any of our special offers. Write to us at the following address for information on our newest releases.

Harlequin Reader Service
U.S.: 3010 Walden Ave., P.O. Box 1325, Buffalo, NY 14269
Canadian: P.O. Box 609, Fort Erie, Ont. L2A 5X3

JULE McBRIDE

BEDSPELL

HARLEQUIN®

TORONTO • NEW YORK • LONDON
AMSTERDAM • PARIS • SYDNEY • HAMBURG
STOCKHOLM • ATHENS • TOKYO • MILAN • MADRID
PRAGUE • WARSAW • BUDAPEST • AUCKLAND

ISBN 0-373-69178-5

BEDSPELL

Copyright © 2004 by Julianne Randolph Moore.

This edition published by arrangement with Harlequin Books S.A.

® and TM are trademarks of the publisher. Trademarks indicated with ® are registered in the United States Patent and Trademark Office, the Canadian Trade Marks Office and in other countries.

www.eHarlequin.com

Printed in U.S.A.

1

"AREN'T PARTIES AT THE MET absolutely fab?" mused C.C.

"Divine," returned Diane.

"Those chicks in *Sex and the City* have got nothing on us," chimed Mara.

"Stick around for just a few more minutes...." As Signe Sargent continued serving cocktails to costumed people sidling up to a makeshift bar, she glanced at her girlfriends, all wearing cat costumes. Through floor-to-ceiling windows behind her, light from the nearly full moon and star-scattered sky poured into the room, illuminating the ancient stone Temple of Dendur, brought from the Nile and reassembled in the Met's Sackler Wing, as part of the museum's permanent collection.

"We'd love to stay—" C.C. reached to adjust the pointed cat ears nestled in her silken shoulder-length hair "—but while our kitty-cat costumes still look fresh, we've got to get downtown to Gus's gig." Gus was the owner of the bar nearest Signe's walk-up in the Village.

Diane, who'd flipped open a compact, was checking her lipstick. "I wish you weren't working, Sig. You could go with us."

"Thanks for sneaking us onto the guest list," put in Mara.

Diane closed the compact, then tilted back a champagne flute, drained it and placed it on the tray beside Signe. "Sneaking in here was risky, but definitely worth it," she pronounced, flashing a business card she'd managed to get from one of the hot, circulating bachelors.

Afraid her boss might recognize her friends' names, since the bash, given by a computer mogul, was strictly for New York's crème de la crème, Signe had signed everyone in under false names.

"It's definitely one of the better parties we've crashed this month," agreed C.C. with a sigh.

"Amazing hors d'oeuvres," added Mara.

After filching another pumpkin-shaped tart from under her workstation, Signe nodded, munching. "I still haven't seen Gorgeous Garrity."

"You will," assured C.C.

Maybe. Signe's eyes settled on the windows behind her opening onto Central Park. In full autumnal glory, the park was beautiful, the trees bursting with color. Gold and russet, they glimmered with night dew and framed a moon so romantic that even the most jaded New York cynic might swoon. It was the perfect backdrop for propositioning Gorgeous. *So, where was he?*

Signe's gaze returned to the cavernous room—the ancient Egyptian tombs, the stone statues of guardian goddesses and the temple itself. As mystical as the moon, Dendur stood just as it had for thousands of years, its yellow stones covered in hieroglyphs.

"I met a Rockefeller," Diane said.

Signe nodded, still scanning the crowd for Gorgeous. While it wasn't generally known, the museum was available for private parties, at least if they were given by the city's movers and shakers. Tonight, faces recognizable from magazines and the news were everywhere.

"I met Ghardi," Mara was saying. "You know? That shoe designer who does the retro-platforms with the gaudy bows on the toes?"

"C'mon, you guys," said C.C. "If we don't get downtown nobody will be left at Gus's, and I want to see the costumes." Greenwich Village's pre-Halloween parade was tonight, and there was bound to be stragglers.

"So many parties," said Diane. "So little time."

"And there will be even more on Halloween night," agreed Mara.

"I'm glad they have the downtown parade early."

Signe pressed a martini into the furry paw of a man in a bear costume, then a cosmopolitan into the black-gloved hand of a witch, and then she glanced between her friends again and grinned, since they all looked so vixenlike in matching black jumpsuits. Tails were pinned to their fannies; they'd found headbands with ears attached; and whiskers were drawn on with black eye pencil. Black masks covered their eyes.

Not that the women looked the least bit alike. C.C. was petite with russet hair she blew so straight that it always looked as if she'd ironed it, while Diane—the one men usually drooled over first—was tall, blond and statuesque. Mara, with her strong, angular bones and clear skin, was good-looking enough to get away with keeping her brown hair conveniently short, eschew makeup and dress in a wardrobe that Diane always termed "grunge-inspired."

"I really wish I could go with you," Signe said regretfully. "Are we still having breakfast tomorrow?"

As C.C. nodded, a hank of reddish hair spilled over her shoulder. "Want to meet at Sarah's on the West Side? They've got those wicked apple tarts."

Everybody agreed.

"And what about the wiccan thing?" asked Signe. Through the business Diane had opened the year before, Wacky Weekends, she offered novelty getaways for bored Manhattanites. She'd just heard of a solstice event in the Catskill Mountains hosted by a group of women from New Jersey. Since the group's monthly gatherings might appeal to her clientele, she'd asked her friends to help her check it out.

"It's this upcoming weekend," said Diane. "So, we'd better firm up our plans."

"I'll rent a car," said C.C., who was the only one of the four women who enjoyed driving.

"Get a convertible," said Signe. "It should still be warm enough."

"Indian summer's going to hold through the weekend," offered Mara. "It said so on the news."

"We'll all chip in for the car," continued Diane.

Signe nodded. "What should we bring?"

"Aspirin," C.C. quipped. "It's rumored that the New Jersey wiccans serve a herbal root beverage that kicks butt."

Diane scoffed. "Forget aspirin. I'll bring Bloody Mary mix."

"And forget your bathing suit, Sig," said Mara. "If it's warm, everybody's skinny-dipping in the lake."

C.C., who hated nature almost as much as Signe, arched an eyebrow. "Lake?" she groused. "What lake?"

"The cabins are on a lake," explained Mara.

Crinkling their noses, C.C. and Signe exchanged glances. Signe said, "That means insect repellent. I think I've got some left over from the last time we were dragged into the wilderness."

"Good. Oh!" C.C. added. "Don't forget to bring something belonging to the man you're casting a spell on. On Saturday night, the wiccans place a boiling cauldron in the center of their magic circle—"

"And we're all supposed to throw in an object while we read a spell that we've written ourselves," said Mara.

"You mean, to make a man fall for you?" asked Signe, thinking of Gorgeous.

C.C., who wasn't the committal type said, "Or have sex."

At that precise moment, Signe's eyes landed on Gorgeous Garrity, who was standing on the other side of the room, and she sucked in a breath. Since leaving Wall Street to take over his father's position, running Garrity Enterprises, a conglomerate that owned businesses around the world, Gorgeous had been on the cover of *New York* magazine, *New York Business World* and *People*. He'd also taken a liking to Signe.

"Speak of the devil," said Mara.

"He's eyeing the bar," observed C.C., her voice hitching. "He's about to come over here, so we'll make ourselves scarce."

Signe glanced downward at her gold blouse and silk pantaloons, then ran a hand nervously over the shoulder-length black wig that framed her heart-shaped face, hoping Gorgeous would like the Cleopatra costume. Just contemplating a conversation with him made the pulse in her throat tick wildly, and the thought of sleeping with him...

She sighed. "He's so rich."

"Try not to think about it," coached C.C. "Just think of him as an average American male."

But Gorgeous Garrity didn't have an average bone in his body. Each bone, in fact, was long and tailored, just like the sport jackets he wore when he visited the Met during his lunch hour.

"He's definitely heading this way, as soon as the woman in the milkmaid outfit lets go of him...." Diane murmured.

Signe's voice hitched. "Only because he wants a drink."

"*Au contraire!*" scoffed C.C. "As busy as he is with Garrity Enterprises, he doesn't have to come to the museum every day to get a cup of coffee at noon. He does it to flirt with you, Sig."

Signe's thoughts exactly. "He told me to call him George."

All three women said, "George?"

"That's his name."

C.C.'s eyes widened. "I didn't know that."

"Nobody does. Everybody's called him Gorgeous for years."

"Well, he's definitely that," said Mara. "Here he comes!"

"I don't want to read too much into this," Signe said nervously. She was only a waitress in the museum's café. It wasn't exactly an esteem-building job, either. She tried not to compare herself to her girlfriends, but over the past year, she'd watched each of them achieve career ambitions. Diane had opened Wacky Weekends, C.C. had begun taking on her own accountancy clients and Mara had become a Realtor.

But Signe wasn't giving up hope. In college, she'd studied art and library science. While working for the New York public library, she'd kept applying for jobs at the Met with no luck, so she was trying this new tactic. She'd do anything she could to meet the curators and get them to consider her for one of the coveted jobs in the archives department.

She loved everything about this museum. Its dark, gloomy corridors, marble staircases and smell of oil paint all made her heart sing. Just breathing the air inside the cavernous rooms quickened her blood almost as much as Gorgeous Garrity. Spending the past six months slugging coffee and helping at these private parties had finally paid off, too.

Tonight, her boss, Edmond Styles, had told her that one of the archives assistants was quitting. Come Monday morning, when the woman's two-week notice was official, Signe would be offered the job of her dreams. She was so excited. Edmond knew everything about art, and was reputed to have connections with the Garritys, through the museum, since they frequently donated artwork.

Signe took another deep breath. It would be so wonderful if something—even just one sizzling night of sex—would happen with Gorgeous....

It was a fantasy, of course. Just a dream, but who knew? She could feel her own star peaking, bright on the horizon. Sighing with satisfaction, she drifted her gaze over the pagan statues the computer mogul had borrowed for tonight's bash. Most had come from private collectors around the city, and all were displayed on lit pedestals. Yes, she'd done a great job, if she had to say so herself. Tonight, presumably anticipating her promotion, Edmond had entrusted her with the responsibility of logging the borrowed artworks into the archives department, arranging them on the pedestals and even flipping the alarm switch that protected the pieces from theft. From start to finish, this display was her baby.

"Those statues are something to behold," commented Diane, catching her gaze.

"Well hung," added Mara dryly.

Signe grinned. Most of the figurines were fertility gods with noticeably disproportionate male hardware.

Diane pointed, laughing. "I think I dated him once."

"You wish," joked Mara.

C.C.'s voice sharpened. "Here comes Mister Wonderful!"

Signe braced herself. "He's so...out of my league." While her parents were professionals in Minneapolis—her father was a lawyer, her mother a history teacher—their lives were modest compared to Gorgeous's jet-setting lifestyle.

"Don't sell yourself short," said Mara. "You've got that Winona Ryder thing going for you."

"True." Everybody thought she looked exactly like the movie actress. "But that might not be a plus. "She was arrested for shoplifting, remember?" Signe said nervously.

"That was years ago," Diane assured.

Signe barely heard. Her knees weakened as Gorgeous came nearer. He was definitely...well, gorgeous, dressed as a seventeenth-century courtier. A richly embroidered purple cape swirled over a white doublet with a standing ruffled collar. A sword was strapped to his narrow hips, and it thrust from beneath the cape, its sheathed length brushing tight breeches. Signe's eyes riveted to the pants fly, which was tightly laced over a bulge that the man was hardly bothering to hide.

All three women blew out a shaky breath in unison.

C.C. softly whispered, "You go, girl."

Realizing that every muscle in her body had tightened, Signe forced herself to inhale as she lifted her gaze, taking in the rakish white-blond wig that hung to his powerful shoulders. He was wearing a conical velvet hat in lush purple.

"Well, we're off, Sig," whispered C.C.

"Don't forget to get something from him," coached Mara. "His pen. Or a lighter."

"Something you can throw into the wiccan's cauldron," said Diane.

At the thought of casting a spell on Gorgeous Garrity, Signe felt pin prickles actually rise at her nape. Should she cast a spell to marry him, she wondered, or just have sex? "Casting a spell won't work."

"Probably not, but it's worth a try," said Mara.

C.C. was scissoring her fingers in a goodbye wave. "See you in the morning at Sarah's. Let's make it ten o'clock."

Eyes on Gorgeous, Signe nodded. "See you."

Her heart was still hammering when Gorgeous leaned casually over the bar a moment later. Somehow she managed to find her voice. "What can I get for you?" She paused. "George."

He flashed a dazzling, hundred-watt smile that was like something straight out of the movies. "You can get me out of here," he said confidentially. "If I'm accosted by one more milkmaid who wants a date, I'm going to scream."

As Signe strained to hear him over the beating of her own heart, she vaguely wondered at the power this man seemed to wield over her. "Get you out of here?" she echoed. "Where would you like me to take you?"

"Where a woman like you could," Gorgeous said with an easy grin. "We could start with heaven and just take it from there."

When it came to flirtation, the man had a thousand smooth moves. Every time he got this close to her, Signe felt like Cinderella. Right now, she'd almost chuck her life dream of working at the Met, just to drag him into the cloakroom and divest him of his costume. Who cared what her boss would think? Despite her nervousness, she shot Gorgeous what she hoped was a game smile. "Well, you've got to admit that the art's interesting."

"Very. I think my uncle Harold lent Jack some pieces." Jack was the computer mogul.

As Signe tried to imagine a life in which one lent others personally owned priceless artifacts for parties, she glanced around, noting the number of cute, costumed kids who'd been brought to the party by their parents. "Really?" she managed to say.

He nodded. "Among them, the statue of Eros."

Her cheeks warmed. Given the elongated penis of the fetish, she didn't exactly want to stare at it, but then, she didn't want to glance away too quickly, either. If she did, Gorgeous Garrity might think she was what her friends accused her of being—a prude. "I read about Eros in an art history class," she said, returning her eyes to Gorgeous Garrity's, which were blue and sparkling. "They say it brings sexual potency to whomever possesses it." Just saying the word *potency* while staring into such astonishing eyes made her feel giddy.

His lips curled in a half smile as if to say he was well aware of the fact. "Really? Well, maybe so. Uncle Harold's been married more than once."

"Reproductions of the statue are sold in the gift shop. They do a booming business."

"Even a reproduction may ensure great sex?"

"Apparently."

His smile broadened. "Do you have one?"

"A statue of Eros?" Her heart missing a beat, she vaguely wondered how she should respond. Imagining Gorgeous in her Village apartment, naked and between the sheets, had occupied most of her dreams lately. Still, despite her girlfriends' endless admonishments that she should loosen up, she didn't want to give the impression that she was easy. She had no doubt that women flung themselves at Gorgeous Garrity all day. "No," she finally admitted. "No Eros reproductions. I can, however, offer other types of potency."

Gorgeous looked very intrigued.

Lifting a wine bottle, she raised an eyebrow in question.

He considered. "What about a Stoli and tonic instead?"

"Coming right up." As she fixed the cocktail, her eyes slid over his costume. Most removable items—the sword, hat and belt—were too large or too hard to get for the purposes of the spell she meant to cast on him. She could borrow a pen, or ask for a business card....

Her eyes settled on the edge of a red silk handkerchief tucked in his waistband. Just looking at him, she shuddered. He was big all over. The kind of guy who, naked, would be covered with silken curling hair—all dark blond in his case. His legs were bunched with muscle, probably from playing polo, which Signe knew he enjoyed. He flashed her a smile.

She smiled back. She simply couldn't believe it. Before she'd started this harmless flirting with Gorgeous, she'd never had sex on the brain—at least not like this. She considered herself sexually healthy, of course, but usually, when it came to men, she was much more practical. Gorgeous, despite his bank account and prospects, had looks that made her nerves quiver.

Schooling her hand not to shake, she gave him the drink, then she stepped back and feigned a sneeze. Without hesitation, he lifted the red handkerchief from his waistband and pressed it to her palm. Making a show of blowing her nose, she smiled. The ploy had worked like a charm. "Why don't I launder this?" she suggested. "I'll keep it here for you, since you come in so often."

"And you're always here," he returned with another of those smiles that made her feel as if she was the only woman in the room. "Don't they give you time off?"

This was his entrée! Was New York City's most eligible bachelor really going to ask her out? "Actually, yes, they do. I'm going to the Catskills this weekend."

"Whereabouts?"

"The state park. An area called the Clover Fields."

"Sounds lucky."

Was he asking if *he* could get lucky? "Maybe." She giggled. "I'm in cabin seven, too. Isn't that a lucky number?"

"It sure is."

The cabins only slept three, so she'd decided to let her girlfriends stay together while she was to share with a roommate—one of the New Jersey wiccans—whom she hadn't yet met.

It might have been her imagination, but Gorgeous's eyes looked veiled. "Going alone?"

"With girlfriends." When he looked disappointed, she took a deep breath and plunged on. "Unless you decided to show up."

"Me? Show up?"

She wasn't sure if she'd made a mistake. "You know, if you were in the area."

As if he just so happened to pass the Catskill Mountains every day of the week, he smiled and said, "You know, I just might run into you."

His eyes locked into hers then. They were the same blue as the ocean under a burning sun hung in a cerulean sky. Breath left her lungs, and full years could have passed before she managed to blink. When she did, it was only because someone in the room had screamed.

"What was that?" she managed, tearing her eyes away.

"The statue of Eros!" shouted the voice as if in response to her question.

Her heart pounding with worry, she shifted her eyes to the pedestal on which the artifact had been displayed moments before, and then she blinked, feeling as if she was watching her life flash before her eyes. She saw Edmond Styles snatching away her promised promotion into the archives department. For a moment, wishful thinking almost made her believe the statue was still there. She could almost see it—about a foot tall, carved of dark wood.

And then she whispered, "It's gone!"

THE NEXT MORNING, with only a day left until Halloween, Signe found herself shifting uncomfortably in a
roller chair in the Met's boardroom when Detective
Alfredo Perez from the Eighty-fourth precinct
stopped pacing to cast a suspicious glance toward the
overnight bag at her feet. He was tall, pencil-thin,
with short, spiky dark hair, ink-black eyes and a handlebar mustache that Signe thought made him look
like a Mexican thief from an old spaghetti western.

Not taking his eyes from her bag, he said, "I was
going to tell you not to leave town."

Not a good sign. "Am I under arrest?"

He didn't bother to answer. "Where are you going?"

She wasn't sure she should admit it. "A wiccan retreat."

"Wiccan?"

"Uh...you know. Witches."

"Ah," he said. "You're a witch, then?"

Great. She could see the wheels turning. Detective
Perez was connecting this information with the stolen
statue, which was pagan. "No, actually, I'm not." She
lunged into a quick explanation of the trip and finished by flashing a smile and intoning, "I do not
know, nor have I ever known, any real witches."

He wasn't amused. "What about cats?" He slid a
grainy photograph toward her, probably reproduced
from a security video. It was of her at the bar, talking
to C.C., Diane and Mara. Signe hedged. It was bad
enough that they thought she hadn't turned on the
alarm, even though she knew she'd done so, but

she'd definitely be fired if she admitted to signing friends into the party under fake names.

"I know I turned on the alarm."

He eyed her a long moment. "Who are these women?"

The man's distrustful attitude was beginning to unnerve her. "I don't know." Surely, it would be proved that she'd flipped the switch on the alarm. If so, she'd be in the clear. Besides, her friends weren't involved in the theft, and a priceless statue was bound to be found quickly, right? "Whoever took the statue will try to sell it," she ventured. "Won't they? I mean, don't you think it will show up on the black market...?" Noting the pleading tone in her own voice, she let the remark trail off.

"Maybe."

She took that for a yes, and sighed in relief. No, she wasn't about to jeopardize her future at the museum by admitting she'd added her friends to a private party's guest roster, just so they could grab some free drinks, catered hors d' oeuvres and meet some good-looking rich men.

Detective Perez was staring at her coldly. "What were these cats talking about?"

She thought fast. "Mostly volunteer work." That sounded positive and upbeat.

His voice sharpened. "And they were volunteering...?"

"I'm not exactly sure," she managed to say. "But it was clear they were very nice women. Not the sort to steal artifacts. You know," she continued, the lies not coming easily, "they sounded as if they loved...uh...small children. And pets. I think they even mentioned giving gifts to people less fortunate than themselves."

"Cat burglars," he muttered. "Cute."

Was Detective Perez really considering her friends as suspects? "They seemed like very nice women," Signe repeated.

His eyes pinned her. "You said they didn't talk to you."

"Well—" Her throat constricted, and she swallowed hard. "It was in the way they ordered."

"The way they ordered?"

"They didn't sound like thieves."

"How do thieves sound?"

She searched her brain. "Not like...nice women."

"Our conversation is getting a little circular."

At least he'd noticed. Reaching down, she clutched the handle of her overnight bag. As she did, she thought of Gorgeous for the first time since the interview had begun. He'd been truly kind after the theft was discovered, and while he'd never again referred to her invitation, she was sure she'd seen something promising in his eyes. Ten to one, he was going to turn up in the Catskills tonight. "Look, Detective Perez, I'd like to help—I really would—and if you need to speak to me again—"

It was the wrong time for her cell to ring. Wincing apologetically, she slid a hand into her purse and drew out the phone. Quickly opening it, she whispered, "Hello?"

"I'm on my way in a fabulous yellow convertible,"

chortled C.C. "I've already picked up everybody else. Be in front of the Met in ten."

As she powered off, Signe wrenched her gaze from the grainy photo of her friends in their cute cat costumes. Detective Perez's dark eyes were still scrutinizing her, and even without a mirror, she knew she looked guilty. Lying had never been her strong suit. When she was little, she'd actually spent hours practicing telling untruths in the mirror. It had never helped. At the age of seven, her own father had made her swear on a Bible he used for his legal work that she'd never attempt to play poker.

"If we're done," she ventured, "I've really got to go."

"One more question."

"What?"

"How's your sex life, Ms. Sargent?"

Her eyes widened. "My sex life?"

"Yes," he said. "Your sex life, Ms. Sargent. It's where—"

Quickly, she raised a hand, murmuring, "Uh...no need to explain." After a stunned moment, she added, "Oh." Was Detective Perez wondering if a lack of potency was her motive? Did he really think she'd stolen the statue of Eros to enhance her life in the bedroom?

Heat flooded her cheeks. "It's..." *Virtually nonexistent right now, except for my dreams about Gorgeous Garrity.* "Fine," she said decisively. "No problems there." Unless you considered that her mother called every Thursday night like clockwork to see if she'd met "a nice young man," which meant someone professional and well employed, with a bright future.

Before Detective Perez could asked any more embarrassing questions, Signe lifted the overnight bag, butterflies taking flight in her belly as she thought of Gorgeous Garrity's handkerchief, which was tucked next to her panties.

Just as she reached the door, the detective said, "Has anyone ever mentioned that you look like Winona Ryder?"

"Yes." Plastering an innocent smile on her face, she felt sure the wheels in his brain were spinning once more, and that he, too, was making the shoplifting connection. "They have." For good measure, she added the word "sir."

Sighing in relief, she exited the archives department and followed the few remaining tourists who were being shunted toward the revolving front doors. She was going to be late to meet her friends now. Rounding the grand staircase, she glanced upward, her eyes suddenly stinging as they settled on the Tiepolo painting in the upstairs gallery. What if her dream to work here didn't materialize?

It had to. She loved everything about this place. The press of the crowds. All the tourists. How the scary, long, dark corridors went on forever, fading into shadowy marble staircases. She'd wanted nothing more than to spend the rest of her life in this building, cataloging artifacts, but now she—not to mention C.C., Diane and Mara—was a suspect in a heist. Things couldn't get much worse. Or at least she thought so before she heard Edmond Styles behind her.

"Signe?" he called. "May I have a word?"

Definitely ominous. Taking a deep breath, she kept her eyes on the security guards stationed before the brass revolving doors opening onto the autumn sunlight, then she forced herself to turn around. "Of course, Mr. Styles."

"I'm so sorry," he said solemnly. "But I just spoke with Detective Perez, and until this matter is cleared up, we're going to have to let you go."

"LOOK AT THE BRIGHT SIDE," Diane whispered philosophically.

"What bright side?" Signe considered herself a cup-half-full person, but she hadn't yet found one. It was hours later and the women were standing in a clearing in the woods, surveying a magic circle fashioned from broomsticks laid end to end.

Between sips of spiked herbal-root beverage, Diane kept her voice to a hushed whisper, so as not to upset the more earnest witches in attendance. "If you're fired, Sig, you can spend next week helping me with the Manhattan Men program."

"You've got a point," admitted Signe.

"You'll be on the payroll, and it will cheer you up."

Manhattan Men, the program Diane was offering through her business, Wacky Weekends, was an intensive week-long experience designed for businessmen who had more money than culture, and who wanted to learn how to present themselves with more class. Next week was the program's test run, and so far, six men from around the country had signed up. Their dates—C.C., Mara and Signe, as well as some other friends—would show the rich bachelors how to impress business associates. Between learning how to dress, order in restaurants and select fine wines, they were in for a week long extravaganza that would include trips to art openings, operas and high teas.

"Mara and I are taking vacation time, so we can participate," reminded C.C.

"Sounds good," Signe managed to say, still upset over the work suspension, and took another sip. The herbal-root beverage definitely had a bite. She frowned. "What do you think is in this?"

Diane didn't hesitate. "Pure grain alcohol."

Doubtful, Signe thought. She rarely drank. "It doesn't taste like it."

"You wait," said C.C. darkly.

For once in her life, Signe decided she might not really mind tying one on. Besides, Gorgeous hadn't stopped in on his lunch hour, as he usually did, but then maybe that meant he planned to surprise her tonight. She sighed. In the car, on the drive to the mountains, a heated debate had taken place, and all the women decided not to speak to Detective Perez and see how things played out over the next week. If the thief still wasn't caught and Signe wasn't reinstated in her job, then they'd reconsider their strategy. Despite stories and movies to the contrary, they'd reasoned, priceless artifacts rarely really vanished. Surely, they were too hard to sell. All they had to do was wait for the police to find Eros.

C.C. knocked back her herbal root beverage, then fanned herself. "It's hot out here."

"Remember last Christmas?" said Diane. "It was seventy degrees."

"Global warming," explained Mara. "At least we can skinny-dip in the lake after the ceremony."

The ceremony. Signe's eyes settled on the huge black kettle in the center of the magic circle. Beneath it, a fire roared. Reaching into the back pocket of her cut-offs, she withdrew Gorgeous Garrity's handkerchief and the spell she'd written. "It's not very good," she whispered. Since it concerned Gorgeous, she'd meant to spend quality time on it, but her concern over the missing Eros statue and Detective Perez's sudden entrance into her life had distracted her.

"You really can't expect yourself to write a good spell," Diane commiserated, "not when so much is going on in your life, Sig."

So true. Wishing she'd done a better job, she moved up in line, watching Mara. Following the protocol of the New Jersey wiccans, Mara removed one of the brooms, which was functioning as a gate. After opening the symbolic door, she closed it behind her and walked toward the boiling cauldron. When she reached the pot, she tossed in a jock strap that had belonged to her ex-boyfriend, Dean. Even though the breakup had been definite, he still wouldn't quit calling. Unfolding the spell she'd penned, Mara began to read:

"Dean, I hate to be unkind
But it seems I haunt your mind.

Oh, SoHo man I've left behind,
May this spell break our binds..."

"Get ready," C.C. whispered. "You're next, Sig."

Signe nodded, taking one more anxious glance around. While Minneapolis had its share of sprawling state parks in the middle of the city, she'd never frequented them. She was a city girl, born and bred. The woods made her nervous. She found herself thinking of insects. Wildcats. Bears. You name it. Her imagination always ran wild.

Fortunately, tonight, the herbal beverage was mitigating her anxiety. In fact, the more she drank, the more she got a warm, fuzzy feeling deep in the pit of her stomach. Right now, the rustic log cabins that were barely visible through the tall trees looked inviting, even though Signe's roommate had canceled at the last moment, since one of her kids was sick. That meant Signe was going to wind up sleeping in a cabin all by herself. Not that she couldn't join her friends, but the beds were single and it would be uncomfortable.

Being alone would be fine, she told herself. It was safe. No men were around. Regarding the retreat, most of the women looked less like witches and more like soccer moms from New Jersey who wanted a girls' night out, away from their husbands and kids.

Diane's elbow caught her in the ribs. "Mara's done, Sig. You're next."

Miming Mara's movements, she, too, headed for the circle. Using a broom as a gateway, she entered the magic area, then replaced the broom and approached the cauldron. A wave of heat hit her, warming her cheeks as she peered over the edge. Floating under the bubbling surface, she could make out a pager, a cell phone and a Brooks Brothers tie. The jilted fiancée of a dentist had dropped in his Water Pic, after reading a spell that included the words: "You thought I was the hostess with the mostess. Now I'm wishing you halitosis."

One overzealous redhead had tossed in the keys to her husband's Lexus, realizing too late that she'd borrowed his car to come to the retreat. Another had offered the last lock of her boyfriend's hair before he'd gone prematurely bald, in the hopes that his hair would grow back.

Signe took a deep breath. Shutting her eyes, she conjured an image of Gorgeous Garrity, and for a blissful moment, she forgot all about the missing potency statue, Detective Perez and the fact that she was—hopefully temporarily—unemployed. What if Gorgeous did come to the mountains tonight? She breathed out shakily, imagining how his hands might feel on her body.

Their conversation had been preempted by the theft of the statue, but before that, Gorgeous had sounded as if he was seriously considering a trip up here. Turning toward the wiccans, she cleared her throat, straightened her shoulders and read:

"O, ye spirits, do hear me
In a crystal ball do see
An eve of sexy revelry
With a man I call Garrity

And if we should be good in bed
I beseech ye, we should wed
And now that this has all been said
I give this handkerchief of red."

Turning, she dropped the handkerchief into the boiling water, then had the strangest falling sensation, as if a rug had been jerked from beneath her feet. Her breath caught as it went under the bubbling surface of the water, the pointed tail of it swirling once before it was lost.

Surely it was nothing—just fanciful thinking, as if the spell might work—nevertheless, the hairs at her nape were prickling her warm skin when she exited the circle. The feeling lingered as Diane cast a spell to make her business, Wacky Weekends, thrive, and as C.C. angled for another promotion. Only when the women began stripping and running into the lake did the feeling start to dissipate.

As C.C. pulled a sundress over her head and weighted it down with a rock, Signe said, "wouldn't it be kind of creepy if these spells really worked?"

Mara was wiggling out of her shorts. "Creepy?"

Signe shook her head. "I don't know," she murmured. "Back there, I got this...weird feeling. Like it was real. Like it's going to work."

"And you're going to marry Gorgeous Garrity?" asked Diane.

"Or just sleep with him?" asked C.C.

"You wish," chimed Mara. "C'mon, get undressed."

That changed the subject. "I'm not swimming in that lake."

Mara shot her a long look. "Why, may I ask?"

Signe laughed. "Because when I free-associate, lakes make me think of words such as rocks, fish and slime."

"No excuse," declared C.C. "If I can do this, you can."

"What the heck," Signe said on a sigh, stripping off her shorts and panties, and glancing around as she downed the last gulp from her pewter mug. "What if someone sees us?"

"There's nobody out here," assured Diane.

C.C., wearing her bra and panties, grabbed her friends' empty mugs and said, "I'm getting us all refills before I get in."

The stuff was definitely tasty. Usually, Signe didn't indulge much, but her friends were right. This was a girls' night. No men were in the woods. And the lake really was beautiful, the crests of its softly lapping dark waters glinting with light from the glowing full moon. If Gorgeous Garrity really did show, he probably wouldn't mind if Signe was just a little tipsy....

The alcohol seemed to be making her quite bold.

"Make mine a double, C.C.," she suddenly called.

And then she pulled off her panties and, tired of the other women teasing her for being relatively body conscious, she made a point of throwing the scrap of silk to the night breeze. As a gust of wind caught her underwear, Signe ran for the water.

Which meant her back was turned when C.C. returned with the drinks and pulled the age-old camp joke of hiding the rest of Signe's clothes.

2

"WICCANS," JAMES MUTTERED derisively. They'd kept him awake half the night. The park ranger yanked the sheet toward his bare shoulders. Every month, he braced himself for another full moon—and their meetings. Half the women were man-haters who tried to place curses on men they'd once loved, and the other half were determined to charm men to the altar, the one place James had vowed never to go.

Even worse, this month the women had arrived right on the heels of James's Wildcat Capture Team certification test, and he'd wanted to spend tonight celebrating. Alone. With only Mother Nature for company. He'd meant to work on the mystery novel he was writing, too, but that had turned out to be a no-go, because of the noise outside.

At least he'd passed the wildcat test. Cats had become a real problem in the park lately, and if you didn't know what you were doing, you could get hurt capturing them. One ranger nearly had his eyes clawed out; another got cat-scratch fever, which James had never thought was a real illness until now. As it turned out, it was caused by bacteria transmitted by cats. Yes, indeed. You definitely had to watch out for felines.

Just this morning, James had caught a mama with six kittens and hauled them down to the animal-habitat people who would find homes for them. Over the past few weeks he'd wound up keeping two that had gotten into fights in the woods. Both of them looked domesticated, and James hated the fact that their owners had brought them to the park to dump them. Why he had such a soft spot for strays, he'd never know, but maybe it was because he was a black sheep in his own family.

As the orange tabby jumped onto the bed, James blew out a perturbed sigh. Even in the dark, he could tell by how its paws hit the sheets that it wasn't the smaller black kitty. "Show some mercy," he muttered, even though there was clearly no hope tonight where sleep was concerned.

The wiccans were still out there, hooting and hollering, which meant he was going to have a real cleanup job tomorrow. The items these women left after they'd cast spells on their poor, unsuspecting targets was enough to chill any man's blood. Wristwatches. Money clips. Television-remote channel changers. Once he'd even found a Swiss Army knife, which, given his attachment to the one he'd carried since his teen years, had seemed like an unusually low blow. Wasn't anything sacred to these women? he wondered.

Every month, as he cleaned the park, he would count his lucky stars that he'd never gotten married. On that score, fate had been most kind.

Sex, of course, was another matter. A man could never get enough sex. And James had to admit that the wiccan women always looked tempting when they got loopy on the herbal-root beverage they made every month, and then jumped into the lake naked. Suddenly, he squinted. Speaking of the lake, had he just heard something drip? It sounded like...

Water? Stifling a groan, he pressed his face farther into the pillow, deciding it was just his imagination. Or the night breeze. Maybe it was starting to rain.

Then he heard it again, just a faint plip-plop. Tilting his head, he glanced in the direction of the sound. It was definitely water. Had one of the cats gotten into the kitchen sink? Maybe. They kept trying to drink from the tub faucet. Rolling, James tried to see into the room. There was a full moon outside—a haunting, romantic full moon of the sort that might conjure werewolves and vampires for the Halloween night—but the curtains were closed against it, and the blinds drawn, so the room was pitch black.

His voice was husky with sleep. "Is somebody there?"

All at once, the plip-plop sounds ceased. The night turned silent except for the sounds of the woods that he loved, the whir of insects and the rushing breeze. He heard an owl hoot.

And then somebody hiccoughed.

"Uh..." He blinked. "Who's that?" He hadn't heard the door to his cabin open. Was one of the wiccans lost? A Cheshire grin made his mouth broaden. Ah. Maybe it was his lucky night, and the blonde who'd stopped earlier, asking for directions...

A sexy, singsong voice called out, "Hello, gorgeous."

Yep. It was definitely the blonde. He listened as Ms. Plip-Plop neared, heading toward the bed. And him. As her steps stilled and her body made contact with the mattress, he sensed, rather than saw, that she was naked. He had no idea how he knew that was true. She just *sounded* naked. He listened more carefully as her bare skin brushed against the sheets.

"Uh...are you lost?" he asked in a sleepy croak.

No answer. Something metallic hit the wood of the bedside table. Had she removed a ring? If so, she probably hadn't come here for idle chitchat. Good. His breath caught as anticipatory heat tunneled through his veins. No doubt, this really was the blonde who'd stopped by the ranger station earlier, asking for directions. He could swear he'd just caught a whiff of that enticing musky perfume she'd been wearing. The woman had been driving a refurbished Mustang, and while she'd been coy about not divulging her name, she'd flirted with him for a full half hour before heading to the parking area designated for the wiccans.

Still blinking sleep from his eyes, James scratched his chest. "Since you're up," he murmured throatily, "why don't you switch on the light? It's by the door." He'd love to get a look at her.

There was a long silence. For a second, he could almost imagine that the woman had disappeared. Or that he'd been dreaming, after all. But no...she giggled again. Just the sound was enough to make him smile. It was a giddy, high-pitched schoolgirl's giggle, and it didn't take a state trooper with a Breathalyzer to figure out that she'd imbibed plenty of herbal-root punch.

"I like the dark," she whispered.

"The dark's good," he conceded. Yeah. It had to be the blonde. Who else would come into his cabin this way?

"And it is very, *very* dark in here," she slurred. When her voice hitched with excitement, it seemed clear that having sex with him was high on her list of priorities, which was fine with him. There was nothing James loved more than being on a woman's "to-do" list.

His eyes narrowed. "How much have you had to drink?"

"Why?"

"Because as tempting as you are, I'd draw the line if you're about to do something you might not do stone cold sober."

She hiccoughed loudly. "What a gentlemen."

"Not really. But I do like a consenting partner."

Her voice turned reedy, catching with promise. "So, you want me to consent?"

"Yeah."

"I do, gorgeous," she murmured solemnly.

For a second, everything went silent, as if the room itself had suddenly inhaled a sharp breath. Yes, this cinched it. Sex was on her agenda. The heat in James's veins started localizing, pooling in his belly, teasing his groin and making him strangely conscious of the hairs on his bare legs, then the tingling between them.

Half asleep, he remembered how she'd looked earlier when she'd gotten out of her car to ask directions.

Her short silken hair had been the color of freshly harvested wheat, and it had lifted with the breeze, while the strong sunlight had done wonders for the rest of her, outlining her nipped-in waist and the gentle flare of her hips. She had sweet, enticing slopes of breasts, and each time she'd moved, rays of light had shined through her blouse, looking like fingers caressing her as the breeze ruffled the fabric. As he sucked a breath through his teeth, James's mouth dried. When he'd gotten into bed tonight, getting lucky had been the last thing on his mind....

He waited for her to make another move.

Every month, these wild women came tearing into the park, their engines roaring, shouting ribald comments and tossing back drinks like sailors. The next morning, they were always hungover. Usually, they decamped as quietly as church mice, as if something so much as turning on the car radio might make their heads explode. They always left, swallowing down aspirin and leaving a wake of lost clothes in the woods. James kept a finders-keepers bin of bras and panties in the main office, but so far, no one had shown up to claim them. This was the first time a witch had actually propositioned him. He couldn't have felt more beguiled.

She was still paused at the edge of the bed.

If he'd known she was coming, he would have changed the sheets, but seeing as it was too late, he tossed back the covers, feeling a sleepy stir of air hit his naked body. "Abracadabra," he said, "c'mon in."

Another giggle sounded.

In the darkness, he couldn't see so much as an outline of her body, so he only sensed it when she leaned forward. "Hocus pocus," she teased. As her splayed hand hit the mattress, a water droplet splashed his face.

"You're one wet witch," he said.

And then she stumbled. Uttering a barely audible gasp of surprise, she lurched headlong on top of him. If he hadn't reached instinctively and looped his arm around her waist, she would have gone over the other side. As it was, one hand caught her hip, and the other, her arm. Settling her on top of him, it was his turn to gasp.

She was naked. Clammy. She sucked in a breath and murmured, "I'm so sorry," but she didn't really sound sorry about crashing into him. He wasn't the least bit sorry, either. She said, "I'm wet and cold."

"We'll have to warm you up."

Every lake-drenched inch of her was searing into him. "You've been swimming," he said, his voice lowering seductively. He couldn't believe that this sexy woman was right on top of him, her breasts cushioning the hard muscles of his chest, the sweet, taut tips of her nipples nestled down in his chest hairs. Her belly was molding to his. And below...

Crisp hairs brushed his thighs, teased the space right below where he most wanted to feel her. The tantalizing crush of her pelvic bone threatened to destroy any shred of reason. James had no idea what he'd done to deserve this midnight gift, but it must have been something good. Probably giving all those kitty-cats homes. Silently, he thanked the goddess to whom these women always seemed to pray. His next shaky breath hit the air, sounding like a whistle.

"I was *swimming* naked, gorgeous," she clarified.

"Sorry I missed seeing you." Just imagining moonlight dancing on her skin was enough to give him another shove toward the edge of sanity.

Her chortling laughter came again. "You don't mind?"

"That you were swimming? Or that you were naked?"

"That I was naked in the park."

Did she think he'd really assert his authority as a ranger and arrest her? "Not in the least," he assured her.

Feeling her body move against his gave him the slightest pause. Earlier, at the ranger's station, he'd thought she was a larger woman, taller and with fuller breasts, but then sundresses could be deceiving, and the airy fabric had swirled around her legs, nearly reaching her ankles. Maybe that had made her look taller. Now he realized she was just a wisp of a woman. Five-five at the most. Had she been wearing high-heeled sandals? He squinted, thinking back to their meeting, trying to remember, but he couldn't....

And then he wasn't even trying. He couldn't think at all. Her mouth came closer; soft pants of breath that smelled like sassafras teased the rim of his ear, and then the enticing moist, pointed tip of her tongue wetted a spot...right before she blew on it. He shuddered. Unable to take her teasing, he lowered his hands on her back, gliding them downward on either side of the most delicate spine he'd ever felt, until he hit her silken backside.

"No panties," he whispered.

"You don't have any panties on, either, gorgeous," she whispered, laughing with another burst of pure hilarity.

He sure didn't. Her splayed hands thrust into his hair, and when he reached up to touch her short locks, he realized they were as wet as the rest of her. As droplets fell from her skin onto his, they heated right up, sizzling as if they were oil hitting a griddle. When her mouth touched his, he knew he was moments from losing the last vestiges of male control. Not that he cared about hanging on to it. He was as hard as a rock, and her slick, waiting heat was calling to him like a siren's song.

"I'm not really a witch," she confessed raspily.

"Could have fooled me."

Thrusting his hands from her nape, up into her hair, he stopped talking and drank in her kiss... deeply...more deeply. The softest lips he'd ever plundered parted under the pressure, and she opened for him, her tongue darting outward and sliding against his. An involuntary moan was wrenched from somewhere deep inside his chest, as if it had been buried there, hidden and lodged inside him for his whole lifetime—until this very moment, when this witchy woman pulled it out.

His mind blanked. He could barely believe this was really happening. He didn't even know her. And yet this felt like so much more than just a kiss with a stranger. Need burst in him. Raw hunger as the open-mouthed kiss turned hotter, wetter and greedier. Electricity that no man would deny was sparking between them. Moaning, he grasped her backside and pulled her closer still, right to his hard, waiting heat. "I want inside," he whispered, his voice strained, completely foreign-sounding to his ears.

Her heart was hammering against his chest. The thought came from nowhere: *one love, one heart.* She said, "Me, too."

Melting, he skated the never-ending kiss downward, from her mouth, to her cheeks, to her neck, and then he shifted his weight, rolling her to her side, so his itching palm could mold her breast.

"Ah," he murmured simply, caressing the silken slope of the underside, then lifting her from beneath and angling down his head to better suckle. After pressing the liquid, searing heat of his mouth to her straining nipple, he used the tip of his tongue to flick it to the bud, then he circled it until her seeking hips were arching; she was silently begging now, for what she'd come here to get.

"Are you sure I'm not dreaming?" he managed to whisper, gliding an open hand down the most succulent body he'd ever felt twining around his own. Wanting to touch each inch of her, he fantasized using his mouth and fingers to make her writhe. "I want to see you wild," he murmured.

"Wild?"

"Yeah." The crazy woman had taken the risk to come in here wet and naked, and now that she'd lit his fire, he intended to make it well worth her while. He definitely didn't want her to walk away, feeling

sorry for her nocturnal visit. Sliding a hand between
her legs, he felt his body boil as his fingers dipped
into her warm, running honey. She was so ready that
he drew in a sharp, satisfied breath…and then he began to probe.

"No—" She exhaled the word, making his blood
dance. He stopped immediately, and she giggled. "I
meant yes, gorgeous."

"You're sure you're real?" He was almost beginning to doubt it. No woman had ever made him feel
so good. And while the blonde had looked promising, this was more than he'd hoped for. Her every
touch was arousing so much more than sexual need.
She was conjuring darker things. Like the need to
possess. To frustrate and toy with her until she was
begging him for satisfaction only he could give.

"I'm real," she said.

"Who are you?"

"You know who I am, gorgeous."

He did. At least he recalled her asking directions.
But he wanted more now. Her name. Her address.
Her phone number. The promise that he wouldn't
wake to find her gone.

Before he could say so, her hand reached down,
sending him crashing into shuddering oblivion as
slender fingers curled around his length. She grasped
him firmly. Stroked. He nearly screamed. Vaguely, he
wondered if she'd said something. He wasn't sure.
The friction of her hand, the way she was rising to
meet the ministrations of his own touch, was more
than he could bear. Each ridge was pleasured, her
nails skimming over flesh until the whole world nar-

rowed focus. There was only her and him. Alone in the middle of the woods on a dark night drenched in moonlight. There was no sound save soft pants as they climbed.

He pulled her back on top of him. Swallowing hard, since his throat was raw, he whispered, "I'm glad you're here."

"I cast a spell on you, gorgeous," she admitted.

"You really think I'm gorgeous?"

"Of course you are," she murmured.

"You cast a spell on me?"

"That's why you're in my bed."

She was in his, but he didn't correct her. Not when he was so flattered. None of these wiccans had ever cast a spell on him before, at least not so far as he knew. "You cast a spell because you wanted to have sex with me?"

"Yes," she murmured, nibbling his lips and groaning as she slid her hands into his chest hairs again. Releasing a moan, he curved his hands slowly over her hips, then down shapely, sexy legs. Fire surged through him once more. Waves of heat seemed to roll through him, only to be drenched by the water still dripping from her body.

"You've got leaves in your hair," he said huskily.

"Take them out."

He did. One by one, he lifted out the dry twigs and brittle leaves that had lodged in her short, wet locks as she'd come from the lake. "You were lucky not to get caught in the brambles," he said, even though his mind was really on the deft movements of her now rolling hips. "Whatever you threw in that cauldron," he added, his lips capturing hers once more, as the damp curve of her belly cradled his, "it's definitely working its charms." Reaching, he stretched an arm toward the bedside table and pulled out the drawer.

She startled, her hands tightening on his shoulders, her nails digging into his skin. He imagined them, how they'd feel moments from now, raking down the rest of his back. This was one wildcat whom he'd gladly let claw him to ribbons.

"What are you doing?" she asked.

"Condoms."

"Good thinking."

"Mere habit," he assured. With her in the bed, any logical thought was truly eluding him. Feeling bereft with her body warmth gone from his, he readied himself, then hauled her back on top of him, simply saying, "Ride me."

Again, that maddening giggle sounded. "Like a broomstick?"

He laughed. "You witch, you."

Her tongue traced his lips, silencing him, sending another shock of awareness through his system. "O, ye spirits bring to me," she whispered huskily, "a night of sexy revelry."

So, that's what she'd asked for. "I think we can manage that."

Her laugh was tempered by need now. "All night?"

"There won't be a thought in your pretty little head until dawn," he assured her, then he added, "I've only got one question."

"What?"

"Well, men and women can do an awful lot of things together," he began. "So, which of those things do you want to do first?"

Her tone was strangely dark, lusty. "You mean, seeing as we're going to eventually do them all?"

"Yeah."

He heard her intake of breath. "Man's choice."

He urged her closer. "You on top, then. And later..." As his words trailed off, everything except the spellbinding woman vanished from James's mind—he forgot his wildcat capture team certification and the hours he'd spend tomorrow, cleaning up after the wiccans—and he touched a thumb to his bedmate's chin, tilting back her head and spiraling kisses down a slender neck that, beneath his tongue, had the smooth consistency of fresh cream.

As her knees bracketed his hips, she exhaled an excited rush of breath. "Later?" she urged as she positioned herself above him and slowly impaled herself, sliding downward on his shaft until he could no longer bite back another moan.

"Everything," he promised hoarsely, seeing himself tongue-kissing every inch of her legs, then burying himself between them, tasting her while she drowned in pleasure. He saw her kneeling before him, too, tasting him with the same abandon. Maybe they'd head outside, right before sunrise, and he'd take her, hard and fast, against a tree, until both of them got so crazy with lust that they'd start howling at the moon.

After all, it was Halloween.

"Sliding down the broomstick," she whispered. He

would have laughed, but he simply couldn't. His blood was pumping too fast, his mind racing with fantasies about the woman who kept calling him gorgeous. The tight, slick folds of her body were enveloping him, stealing away his breath. His arms swiftly circled her back. Squeezing her tightly, he hauled her even closer against him and rolled, so that he was on top of her. Unwilling to simply lie back and take the pleasure, the way he'd initially asked, he realized he wanted to be the one to give it.

"Hold me tight, you wicked little witch," he coached as he thrust deep inside her, feeling her open all the way. "Because the man you've beguiled is about to show you some midnight magic."

WHAT HAD HAPPENED?

Signe slid a hand down her belly, as if she half expected to find that her own body parts had vanished in the night. Whew! That herbal-root punch had really packed a punch. C.C. hadn't been lying! Nor Diane, who'd said it contained grain alcohol. Signe felt as if she'd been run over by a Mack truck. Which was just as well. She'd actually forgotten about the stolen statue and Detective Perez for a few blissful hours. Now she tried to slit her eyes open, but decided it was just too painful. Yes, she was going to have to spend all day pressing thin slices of frozen cucumber to her eyelids.

This was why she never drank. While the herbal-root beverage had been great going down, she now felt as if a heavy cement block had lodged in the space where her head used to be. Except *that* couldn't really be the case, since her head was pounding. It felt as if an army of little men were inside it, trying to bash their way out with hammers.

Everything hurt. A big white hole seemed to exist where her memories once were. It was as if she'd become a cyborg from the movies, whose brain existed only on a CD-ROM. Now she was simply waiting for her memory element to reconnect....

Just opening her eyes hurt. Breathing hurt. Her *skin* hurt.

Everything.

Except the dream. If her lips didn't hurt, too, Signe would have smiled. She'd actually dreamed that Gorgeous Garrity had been waiting for her in bed. She'd whispered the words to the spell she'd cast, and they'd made love. Not just the wham-bam-thank-you-ma'am kind of love, either. But no-holds-barred sex that had lasted all night long.

It seemed so real.

Astonishingly real, she decided with a frown. In fact, the more her memories came back in snatches, the more it seemed as if the event had happened. Was she going crazy? Or had Gorgeous taken her up on her offer and come to the Catskills?

She was still in too much pain to open her eyes.

She could remember his touch, though. Every kiss, every sexy smell. Big strong hands had stroked every inch of her. His hairy chest had teased her breasts in a way that actually made her...have an orgasm?

Yes, he'd barely touched her, and she'd gone off like a rocket. He'd lit her up like a sparkler on the Fourth of July. She'd burned and sizzled.

"Whew!" she mouthed.

As he'd pushed inside her, she'd felt as if a thousand massaging fingers were probing her, driving her toward new, dizzying heights of ecstasy. But that was crazy! Sex was never that good! She was healthy, of course. But a long time ago, Signe Sargent had realized that men were human and had their pretty obvious limitations.

Last night, however...

Had the spell affected their bed play? They'd gotten so down and dirty that just thinking about it made her whole body flood with heat once more. She could almost hear his voice, saying, "I'm about to show you some midnight magic." And boy, had he!

Maybe there was something to this wiccan stuff, she thought, her heart skipping a beat. If it improved sex to this degree, she would certainly become an adept. As soon as she got back to the city, she'd get her own spell book. The dream really did seem so sharp, vivid and full of detail...

She registered a musty smell. "Cats?" she mouthed.

She opened her eyes a fraction. Just enough to see that this wasn't her cabin. Uh-oh. She ceased to breathe, and her aching body felt frozen in panic. Now she couldn't shut her eyes if she wanted to. Where was she? The curtains were different from those in her cabin, she realized, and somebody lived here. Full-time. No...this was no part-time camper, and this somebody was messy.

Without even moving her head, she could tell that the place was a wreck. A closet door was open, and a man's clothes were inside. Not the kind of man's clothes that might have brought her comfort, either, such as Brooks Brothers suits and Hermès ties. This man's shirts were made out of plaid flannel. Yards of it, indicating he was quite sizable.

Dirty jeans were on the floor. Canoe paddles were propped beside the door, near mud-caked steel-toed work boots. An open can of soda was perched on a sofa arm. Not very promising. Had she really walked into the wrong cabin? And slept with some strange man, thinking he was Gorgeous Garrity? And how could such a thing have happened...when her friends swore there were no men out here in the woods?

Her eyes slid to the bedside table, landing on a graduation certificate, and she made out the words: Wildcat Capture Team Certification. Whoever he was, he'd certainly captured her last night.

Feeling desperate for a drink, she took in a desk stacked with books and strewn with papers, and then she saw the disabled cats. Two of them. An orange tabby with its head bandaged and both front paws bound in gauze. The other was missing a leg. Telling herself to remain calm, she pressed a hand to the mattress and tried to roll over. As she did so, she pressed a hand to her head, also. She felt something that didn't belong there and removed it.

"A leaf," she mouthed. Great. More exploration turned up brambles and a twig. Glancing down, she realized her legs were mud-streaked from the swim in the lake. Yes. It was all coming back to her now....

Then he snored.

It was not delicate snoring, the kind C.C. and Diane

could both be guilty of after they'd had too much to drink...the kind that would have assured Signe that she'd wound up in the other cabin with her girl-friends.

No.

This was chesty male snoring that said he was at least six feet tall and packed with muscles of the very type that she'd felt holding her tightly last night. Try-ing not to make a sound, she fought the pain as she craned her neck and glanced over her shoulder.

When she saw him, her heart hammered harder. Who was he? The sheet was pulled only to his thighs, and getting a gander at his physique, she couldn't help but think of the fertility statue Detective Perez thought she'd stolen. No wonder sex had felt so good....

His skin was as smooth as glass and tanned the color of toasted walnuts. He was definitely gorgeous. Just not *the* Gorgeous...Gorgeous Garrity. Which meant she had to get out of here. Escape, while he was sleeping. She'd just run....

But her eyes lingered. He had great hair. Thick and medium-blond, it was decidedly too long; soft curls that had felt like heaven against the insides of her fin-gers were brushing the skin of his shoulders, gleam-ing like summer sun. Faint light, slipping through the closed curtains, was dancing in the strands, and for a brief moment, she watched as if spellbound.

She forced herself to blink rapidly.

Glancing around, she searched for her clothes, then remembered she'd lost them at the lake. She'd come here naked, thinking this was her cabin, and he must have thought...

She was someone else.

Yes. He'd seemed to be expecting her. Great. This was the sort of jam C.C. always got herself into. But nothing such as this had ever happened to Signe. What *would* C.C. do? The answer was just as clear as it had been a moment before: run. *Trust your instincts, Sig.*

Soundlessly, she edged her legs over the mattress, wincing when her feet hit the wood floorboards, making them creak. She glanced over her shoulder again in panic, but the man hadn't moved. So far, so good. Standing, she stared covetously at the sheet on his legs, wishing she could risk taking it, to cover herself. How far was her own cabin from here?

She tiptoed toward the door, wincing as she took a silent step, then another. She was halfway across the room when she heard the groan of mattress springs, and then a gruff voice saying, "Going somewhere?"

She froze, uncomfortably balanced on the balls of her bare feet, her fisted hands at her sides, deeply conscious of the fact that she was naked, and that it was no longer dark in here. Her backside was exposed, and while she didn't exactly want to be a coward, she didn't want to turn around and face him, either.

He said, "You can borrow a shirt if you want."

Her eyes cut to the closet. It was tempting, but if she borrowed a shirt, she'd feel obligated to return it. "Uh...thanks, but I'll manage." Another wave of mortification overcame her when she heard her voice. It sounded weak and gravelly.

"You sure?"

How could he sound so normal? Had he forgotten how they'd spent the better part of last night? She still hadn't managed to move. She'd remained standing in the middle of his cabin, perched on the balls of her feet. Venturing another quick look over her shoulder, she wished she hadn't. The sheer force of the man's over-the-top good looks was—unfortunately— enough to pivot the rest of her body around.

For a long second, she just stared. And then her foggy mind caught up with the rest of her body, and she realized he was seriously checking her out. She crossed her arms over her chest, feeling like an idiot. Casually, she drew one leg in front of the other.

The slightest smile lifted his lips, almost as if he was getting a kick out of her discomfort. She blew out a surreptitious breath, wondering what to do next. His face was strong and broad, framed by blond curls, and his jaw was firm and square, his eyes, the kind of hazel that could turn brown or amber, depending on the light. She felt tempted to crawl right back into bed with him.

Then she remembered the flannel shirts, steel-toed boots and disabled cats. The man might be amazing in bed, but he was not the type with whom a reasonable New York woman could make a lasting future, and Signe was practical. What she wanted most was a future. Reminding herself that she was in enough trouble already, since she was temporarily suspended from the Met, not to mention a prime suspect in the theft of a priceless statue, she edged backward, toward the door.

He huskily said, "I thought you were..."

Someone else. The words hung in the air. Somehow, despite her embarrassment, she managed to keep the smile plastered on her face. "Nope."

His thick eyebrows knitted. "Have we even *met?*"

She really couldn't stand here in front of him much longer, naked. "Nope," she said again.

He slowly sat, pulling the sheet with him, thankfully covering his lower half and bunching the pillow behind him, as if anticipating a lengthy conversation with her, and while she hated to disappoint him...

She'd almost reached the door, but she couldn't help but ask, "And you are?"

"Name's James," he said. For the space of a suspended heartbeat, the whole world slid off kilter and she could swear he was going to add, "Bond. James Bond." But instead he said, "The park ranger."

"The park ranger," she echoed in a hoarse whisper. Of course. How could she have imagined that her magic spell had conjured Gorgeous Garrity? "I see."

He was starting to look offended. "Who did you think I was?"

"Gorgeous," she managed. "I thought..."

He flashed a grin that did remarkable things for his already remarkable face. "Thanks."

"No," she managed to say, realizing he'd thought she was referring to his good looks. "I mean..." But probably it was better not to explain she'd mistaken him for Gorgeous Garrity, a man a park ranger in the Catskills would have never heard of. "I mean...uh..."

He looked flattered. "No need to explain."

Clearly, the man thought she'd noticed him yesterday when she'd arrived for the wiccan retreat, and that she'd decided to sleep with him. "Look," she said, her eyes cutting toward the kitchen and the refrigerator. She licked her dry lips. Right about now, she'd kill for something cold to drink. The guy looked like a Neanderthal, but he'd at least have some orange juice. Still, she needed to get out of here. "It was really nice to meet you, but I...uh, have to go."

"Hmm. Cinderella, you're not even going to leave your name?" His slow, easy, sexy smile said this was merely a formality. After last night, he was sure they'd be seeing plenty of each other. It was tempting, too. But...

"I live in Manhattan," she apologized, "and—"

He brightened. "I'm there all the time."

She had no argument for that. "Uh...Diane Parker-Powell," she quickly lied. "It's listed." Surely Diane would forgive her, and when the guy called—*if* he called—Diane would claim not to know a brown-haired wiccan who'd gotten drunk on herbal root. Call her spineless, but she simply couldn't bear to tell this gorgeous hunk of a man that she didn't want to date him.

"Diane Parker-Powell," he repeated slowly, as if liking the way the name felt in his mouth. His voice rose as she opened the door and backed over the threshold. "I'll call you soon, Diane Parker-Powell."

Guilt flooded her. He sounded so nice. So sincere. And he'd been amazing in bed. *Really amazing.* She didn't want to hurt him. It was just that she'd already planned out her life: first the promotion into archives, assuming she was cleared from the robbery, and then finding a nice professional man of the sort her parents had always expected.

Or Gorgeous Garrity.

Just because he hadn't shown up last night didn't mean the spell hadn't worked, she told herself. Sensing the door, Signe reached her hand behind her and curled her fingers around the knob. Unable to believe she was standing in a strange man's cabin, naked, having this conversation, she forced herself to continue, "To be perfectly honest, I have a huge crush on somebody else. I just got fired...well, temporarily suspended from my job...and I'm a suspect in the theft of a priceless artifact that's reputed to bring sexual potency."

"I see," he said dryly.

"I knew you would," she managed to say.

She opened the door, crossed the threshold and shut it behind her—only to find herself butt-naked on the porch of a rustic cabin in the middle of the woods with no sign of civilization anywhere. From here, she couldn't even see the lake. Or the road. All she could see were trees. Uncertain, she glanced toward the door she'd just closed. What now? She'd assumed all the cabins were grouped together, but apparently not.

She tried not to think about last night, and yet as soon as the man had touched her, she hadn't really been thinking of Gorgeous Garrity, after all. Everything had melted. There were only soft sounds and sensations.

No, she simply couldn't go back inside, she decided, not given this very strange mix-up.

Surely her own cabin couldn't be too far away. And there weren't any other men out here, right? "I mean, it's not like I'm going to run into a bunch of construction workers," she whispered. Nervously, she scanned her eyes around the tree line.

Then she started walking.

3

"WELL, I'LL BE," James whispered, lifting the edge of the window curtain. He peered between the slats of the blind. Last night hadn't been a dream, after all.

The wiccan was real. Barefoot, she was winding her way through the trees, her gleaming backside catching the light of the early morning sun. She'd done some sunbathing this past summer. Even from here, he could still see bikini lines that outlined an incredibly sexy behind.

"Cute," he pronounced. After a moment, he added, "and crazy as a bedbug."

It was just a good thing that Indian summer was holding. Outside, it looked as unseasonably warm as it had been all week. If it hadn't been, she'd be colder than a witch's broomstick. Not that the weather was going to hold much longer. Should he take her a shirt? He had no idea why she hadn't leaped at his offer, especially since her cabin wasn't close. Within walking distance for sure, but he wouldn't want to go even that far without wearing something.

Rubbing the sleep from his eyes, he realized he half expected her to vanish, but she was still moving through the trees like a wood nymph. She also looked like that actress... He thought for a moment, then whispered, "Winona Ryder."

This was Diane Parker-Powell. James decided the name suited her. It had class. She was probably smart, but not in the habit of making it obvious. The way she'd giggled last night, he'd almost taken her for an airhead, but there was more going on beneath the surface. James would bet that somebody had told her men wouldn't find her intelligence attractive. It was a lie he'd be happy to disprove.

Ten to one, she was a librarian, he decided. Or a researcher. Or maybe she worked in publishing. Definitely something bookish. She seemed cerebral, college-educated, probably the child of professionals, but she also seemed pampered, too. Giggly. Like she was used to having loads of fun.

He frowned. She'd said she'd lost her job, hadn't she? "Yeah," he murmured. But it had been hard to listen to her, since she hadn't been wearing a stitch, and he'd wanted nothing more than to pull her back into bed.

Who knew what was truth—and what was fiction? Had she really said she was a suspect in the theft of a priceless artifact? And why? Obviously, Diane had an active imagination, something he'd gleaned from her performance in bed. Had she really cast a spell on him, too? Or was that a lie, also? He sure felt bewitched. As soon as the door had closed behind her, he'd wanted her back. His gut had twisted with something sharp and visceral, as if he'd been about to lose...his soul mate?

Pushing aside the ridiculous thought, he scooped up the tabby and carefully petted around the bandage on her head. How long should he wait before he called her? Or should he skip it?

After all, she hadn't left her number, only said she was in the phone book, and she'd been spouting all those crazy excuses. If her monologue hadn't been so ludicrous, James would have gotten mad. Instead, he chuckled softly as he put the tabby back down on the floor. Not only had she claimed to be a suspect in the theft of a priceless artifact, but she'd also said it brought sexual potency.

"The way you made love," he murmured, recalling her responsive heat. "I could believe it." He could almost see how her back had arched, just like a cat's, her supple spine bending in a sumptuous curve. James wished the lights had been on.

Whistling, he went toward the kitchen, grabbing a box of Meow Mix from the counter. As he gave it a hard, suggestive shake, both the tabby and black kitty came running.

"Here you go. Eat up." Both cats twined figure-eights around his calves before going to the food bowl. As soon as they started eating, James headed for his closet to grab a shirt. He was almost there when his eyes settled on the bedside table. "A ring?"

Plucking it from the table, he scrutinized it. It was a plain silver band with some intricate scrollwork. Was it a wedding ring? Impossible. She couldn't be married! *Not when I just found her.*

Bands seemed to tightened around his chest. All at once, something had seemed to touch a raw nerve; he felt as if he'd kill any man who dared to love Diane Parker-Powell. But that was nuts. She meant nothing to him! Sure, she was great in bed, but it was only a one-night stand. He'd been the black sheep of his family for years because he showed so little promise in terms of making a marriage. He'd never wanted any part of the life that had been mapped out for him. He'd run from home as if the hounds of hell were on his heels. Still...

She was his.

It was that simple. Truly, he could almost believe she'd beguiled him. He tried to laugh off the unwanted feelings, but all that emerged from between his lips was a strained chuckle. Shaking his head to clear it of confusion, he continued to peer down at the ring.

It *could* be a wedding band. However, his gut said Diane wouldn't settle for anything less than a traditional gold band and diamond engagement ring. Why, he didn't know. After all, she'd looked like a wild child moments ago, standing in the middle of his cabin, her skin streaked with lake water, her hair mussed. Still, something in her manner said she'd feel more comfortable in the city, dressed in a suit—and with a man on her arm who had a nine-to-five job.

Settling the ring in his palm, James bounced it lightly, wondering what he should do. If the ring was of value, she was going to wind up driving back to the city without it. Or she might call and ask him to mail it. He could take it to her cabin, but she hadn't left a phone number, so he felt awkward following her. Besides, she really had told him some incredible lies about her life circumstances.

"A suspect in the theft of a sexual-potency artifact," he mused again.

Telling himself he'd had a number of great one-night stands that he'd promptly forgotten, he jiggled the ring in his palm once more and whispered, "Let her come back for it."

"OH NO!" CRIED MARA, tugging a T-shirt downward over her Calvin Klein sleep shorts as she pushed through the screen door of the cabin she'd shared the previous night with C.C. and Diane. "There she is!"

C.C. raced out of the cabin, following Mara, the fingers of one of her manicured hands clutched around a Bloody Mary and the other tightly gripping the collar of a silk robe. "She's naked!"

Diane, who was still tugging on jeans, emitted a startled gasp. "Are you all right, Sig?"

"Were you raped or something?" asked Mara, her face stark white with horror.

"I'm fine," Signe assured.

She wasn't, however. She'd been wandering in the woods for what felt like an eternity, although it had probably been closer to twenty minutes. She felt Mara wrap a hand around her elbow and tug her inside.

Mara said, "Get in here!"

Diane stared. "Where were you? Were you gone all night?"

"Long story," Signe managed to say.

"We have plenty of time," returned a stunned C.C.

"You're safe?" persisted Mara, her eyes wide as she grabbed a dress from C.C.'s suitcase and wrapped it around Signe's shoulders.

"Totally," assured Signe as she slipped her arms through the sleeves and buttoned the garment.

Diane was still gaping. "You look like you slept outside. Did you fall asleep in the woods? Did you get lost?"

C.C. wrung her hands. "I felt so guilty for hiding your clothes."

While she loved her friends, Signe wasn't unaware that the age difference—she was, by two years, the youngest—always brought out their maternal instincts. Sometimes she hated their overly protective attitude. "Of course I didn't get lost," she defended.

"Well...your hair's so messy," countered Diane.

Lifting her drink-free hand, C.C. reached up worriedly and began to smooth it. "We went to look for you, to see if you were packing, but no one was in your cabin!"

"And the bed was made," added Mara.

"It looked as if no one had even slept in it," said C.C.

"We thought you were mad, since your roommate didn't show up last night, and we were all so sorry that we didn't drag another bed in here," continued Diane.

"But then, you said you *wanted* to bunk alone," defended C.C.

Mara peered at Signe carefully. "And when you weren't at the goodbye breakfast—"

"Which was just as well," C.C. quickly put in, "since they only served vegan muffins—"

"What happened to you?" interjected Diane, seemingly anxious to get back to the main topic.

"For a minute, before we read the paper—" Mara said, quickly shifting topics. "Well, we thought your spell really worked, and that Gorgeous Garrity had come up here and—"

"But we knew that wasn't true," assured Mara pragmatically.

"Which was why," continued C.C., "we were about to head up to the park ranger's cabin to—"

Signe's gasp cut her off. "Not the park ranger!"

All the women stopped talking and squinted.

"What's wrong with asking the park ranger for assistance?" queried Diane.

"Especially *that* park ranger." C.C. grinned. "I didn't see him, but last night, the wiccans were saying he was a real babe. Broad shoulders. Terrific tan. Muscles in all the right places. Very nice buns."

"Even if the wiccan gathering hadn't been so much fun—just perfect for one of my Wacky Weekends junkets—it sounded as if I should offer women a trip up here, just so they could see him."

"He'd definitely qualify as a star attraction," Mara agreed. "That's what one of the women from Long Island told me."

"Hotter than the salsa at Lupe's on the Upper East Side," added Diane decisively. "That's what I heard."

Signe took a deep breath.

And then, one by one, she watched the jaws of her friends drop. After a moment, she decided their reaction was offensive. They'd all had one-night stands, after all. Just last month, C.C. had slept with a fireman, a policeman and a chef from Nobu. The month before that, after Mara had broken up with Dean, she'd slept with the first man who'd asked her out—a broker from Morgan Stanley—just to prove she could. Before Diane had begun dating Lou, an artist from SoHo, she'd done her share of catting around, as well.

Yes, the more Signe thought about it, the more she was starting to hate how her girlfriends had pegged her as a prude. So, she said, "You're absolutely right," as she strolled toward the makeshift bar that C.C. had set up on a wooden dresser. As she poured herself a Bloody Mary, something she wouldn't usually do, Signe calmly added, "While you were busy unpacking, I...uh ...met him. He did have very nice buns."

It was an understatement. Just thinking about the man's naked body, Signe felt her tummy tighten. When she turned around to face the group, she was pleased to see they were all staring at her in awe. Mara's lips parted. "You really are a witch. You slept with the park ranger last night!"

Signe mustered a casual shrug, as if to say she did such things far more than her friends would ever suspect, but just had the good grace not to talk about it. "Why not?"

"What happened to kissing on third dates?" C.C. asked dryly.

"And petting only after meeting his parents?" asked Diane.

"And having sex only if he's got an MBA, and the relationship might lead to marriage?" added C.C., seating herself on the edge of an iron bed, looking stunned.

What *had* happened? Even now, Signe wasn't quite sure. All she knew was that the feel of the man's hands hadn't yet left her. He'd had ways of touching she'd never experienced, and she was still aching in all her special places.

"I thought it was time to make some changes," she said, forcing herself to sound decisive.

A laugh escaped C.C.'s lips. "You might start with finding gainful employment."

Mara elbowed C.C. "She's not going to lose that job."

"Don't forget I'm protecting your identity!" said Signe.

"I really wish you all would quit telling me what a prude I am."

"We're only teasing," defended Mara.

"I guess you showed us," commented C.C.

Diane sounded awed. "You really slept with the park ranger?"

"Yes. I did."

"How was it?" asked C.C.

Diane and Mara sat down on the bed, next to C.C. Everyone stared at Signe raptly, while Signe considered. If the truth be told, she felt terrible. Her head was pounding, and the surface of her skin felt sticky and clammy, as if she'd been dipped in refrigerated maple syrup. The last thing she wanted was to drink the Bloody Mary in her hand. The disheveled state of her hair didn't help matters. But her body...

Her body...

Felt wonderful.

She sucked in a breath, and then giggled. "He didn't even mind that I was all wet from the lake."

Diane nodded approval. "Earthy."

"He was." Signe lifted a staying hand. "Not that the relationship is going anywhere. I didn't even give him my phone number." Guilt washed over her when she recalled that, in panic, she'd given him Diane's name. Maybe she wouldn't even tell Diane. Given how crazy she must have sounded—rambling about the statue of Eros—the man wouldn't even call, anyway.

Mara looked even more impressed. "You didn't tell him to call? You just wanted sex, no strings attached?"

"Exactly." It was well known that Signe had her heart set on marrying a professional like her father. "He's a *park ranger*."

"You're a snob," accused Diane, laughing.

Mara elbowed her. "Maybe. But last night, Sig was quite the equal-opportunity seducer."

Signe tried to sound casual. "And it was...great."

C.C. took a deep breath. "You know," she remarked. "This is perfect timing."

Registering that her friends were now exchanging glances, Signe felt her heart miss a beat. "What?"

There was a long silence.

Yes, they were keeping something from her.

Finally, C.C. said, "We've got bad news."

Fighting the sinking feeling in the pit of her stomach, Signe braced herself. This week had been bad enough. The only saving grace had been the few blissful hours she'd spent with James, a man whose last name she didn't even know. "I'm listening."

"You'd better sit down," suggested Mara.

Slowly, she seated herself opposite her friends. They were all as honest as the day was long. When they said bad news was coming, they meant it. Crossing her arms, she waited.

C.C. moved first, reaching behind her. Papers rustled and the *New York Times* appeared. Before C.C. began reading, Signe saw the picture of Gorgeous Garrity wearing a tux. A woman in a bridal dress was on his arm, and both were standing in a garden, beneath a floral arbor.

"Yesterday at three," read C.C., "Christine Van Duren wed George Wilhelm Garrity..."

Numbly, Signe listened to the announcement. Not that she shouldn't have expected it. She'd never even gone on a date with Gorgeous. He was just some rich guy who'd flirted with her, right? Still, he'd shown up at the café counter every day for the past months, and he'd always hung around as he sipped his java, joking with her and talking about art. Signe might be relatively staid with regard to having sex, at least when compared to her friends, but she knew when a man was interested. And he'd definitely been interested.

The news shouldn't have hit her so hard. Especially since she was still floating on air from the sex she'd experienced last night. "So much for the spell I cast," she managed to say lightly, when C.C. set the paper aside.

Her friends were watching her with sympathetic expressions. "Are you sure you're all right?" asked C.C..

Signe considered a long moment. Discounting last night's sexual escapade, of course, this morning capped the most wretched week of her life. She could scratch one life dream, which had been working for the Met. And another, since she'd never marry a man like Gorgeous. She sighed. Well, maybe there had been some validity to her spell, anyway. The sex had been stellar; she'd just found it in the wrong bed. "Yeah," she murmured a smile tilting her lips. "That herbal-root drink was wicked."

"And how!" agreed Sylvia.

Once more, Signe thought of the man's broad chest. His pectorals had been sharply delineated as if carved from granite. The pelt of hair between them had been as soft to touch as mink. Recalling how it had felt to lie on top of him made her nerve endings frazzle. Her headache vanished, if only for that moment. Just thinking about him worked on her hangover like a magic potion. Too bad she couldn't bottle his substance as a "morning after" cure. "Sometimes a girl has to settle," she admitted, chuckling. "If only for a few hours."

"I couldn't have said it better myself," agreed C.C., looking relieved at how Signe had taken the news about Gorgeous.

Mara exhaled slowly, as if she'd been holding her breath. "Why don't we pack and head back to the city. If we hurry, people will still be serving brunch."

Diane nodded. "And we can be injected with an antidote to those vegan muffins."

"I'm up for something starchy," seconded C.C. "And eggs and bacon."

"Something with lots of cholesterol," agreed Diane.

All three looked at Signe. "Are you game?"

She nodded, thanking her lucky stars that a night of wild sex with the park ranger had primed her, making her able to absorb the disappointing information about Gorgeous—and the fact that she'd never have sex with, much less marry a Garrity. She nodded briskly. "Absolutely," she said.

4

A WEEK LATER, JAMES PAUSED on the sidewalk in Manhattan, checking out Wacky Weekends, the business owned by Diane Parker-Powell. The place was just as interesting as it had looked when he'd found it on the Internet. It was down in the Village, on Barrow Street, on a block of brownstones. Lush green plants overflowed in the windowsills and bulletin boards displayed brochures. Leftover Halloween decorations remained—spiderwebbing and cutouts of bats.

Probably he was doing the wrong thing, but Diane had never called about the ring, the way he'd expected, and since he had to come into the city, anyway...

"She owns her own business," he murmured. He'd figured she was smart. And Wacky Weekends, with its creative concept, showed real flair. Novelty travel was bound to appeal to Manhattanites. As his father always said, "You need to make a product people want to buy." James browsed the ads. One boasted urban day tours for out-of-towners. Another promised to whisk overworked women to week-long spas.

He glanced around, then down at the jeans and plaid flannel shirt he wore with a hooded sweatshirt jacket, then he sighed. A leather-clad woman passed behind him just as a businessman in a two-thousand-dollar suit hailed a taxi. A woman wearing a gold muumuu was walking an intricately shaved dog that looked less like a poodle and more like shrubbery topiary. Every time James came into the city, he was stunned at how much attention people paid to style.

He headed for the glass door and went inside. A bell jangled and a petite woman with shoulder-length blond hair who was seated behind the desk glanced up, smiling warmly. "May I help you?"

He nodded. "I'm looking for Diane Parker-Powell."

"Ah." She rose, circled the desk and extended her hand. "That would be me. What can I do for you?"

He was so stunned that he failed to take her hand for a beat too long. Just as she began to withdraw it, he found his manners and extended his own, which made for a very awkward greeting. "Uh..."

He'd been prepared for a great number of scenarios. Especially since she'd left a ring. He'd braced himself for the possibility that she was married, even as he told himself he didn't really care, but it hadn't once crossed his mind that she'd lied about her name.

Now he wasn't sure how he felt. Angry, yes. But he was even more concerned that he might not see her again. This past week, memories of her had haunted him, ghosting through his consciousness. Images of her would flash into his mind all day, and he'd see her standing in his cabin naked, trying unsuccessfully to cover her breasts.

Or he'd recall how she'd looked, mooning him as she'd walked through the woods to her cabin. Diane Parker-Powell—the *real* Diane Parker-Powell—was leaning forward, peering at him. She said, "Are you okay? You look like you've seen a ghost."

"Dandy," he said.

Her features, which had been all scrunched up, as if she was thinking too hard, suddenly relaxed. "Oh, I understand now," she said.

"You do?" he managed to say.

She gave him a once-over, taking in his jeans, flannel shirt and work boots. "You must be here for our Manhattan Men program."

He was still wondering how he was going to find the woman he'd slept with, so his mind couldn't keep up. "Manhattan Men?"

Pointing down, she tapped a manicured finger on the brochure on her desk. "Yes," she said, her smile broadening, her tone inviting. "Don't worry. Everyone feels a little funny at first, but there's no reason to. You're in luck. All the spots were full, but another date mate's just...uh...had a break in her schedule. So, she's free to come in at the last moment."

"Date mate?" What had he gotten into? And why had the woman he'd slept with given him this name? She must have some connection to the real Diane Parker-Powell...but what?

"Yes," she assured. "The woman, Signe Sargent, is a personal friend of mine, and you're going to love her."

"I'm sure the program you're offering is wonderful, but I think I've made a mistake and—"

"At least look at our brochure," she interrupted, looking unperturbed. "In only one week, we guarantee you'll feel much more comfortable while entertaining business associates."

Business associates? How could he politely say he did not have—nor intend to have—business associates. Every move he'd made, from not going to the college of his parents' choosing to working odd jobs, was calculated to ensure he'd never work at a desk.

"Now, as you probably already know, the program's not inexpensive," she was saying, "but I assure you, it'll be well worth it. We've got a big-time cattle rancher flying in from Wyoming. An owner of coal mines is coming from West Virginia...." He barely heard. He just couldn't believe it. Had the woman he'd slept with really vanished? Leaving only one stray item behind, like Cinderella? James shoved his hands deep into the pockets of his jeans. In the bottom pocket of one, he could feel the folded envelope in which he'd put the ring. "Nothing personal," he said, "but there's nothing I hate more than culture."

"I understand," she soothed. "All our clients share your feeling. That's why they're here. And yet, when your pocketbook starts demanding that you hobnob with the elite, a man needs to be prepared."

He was starting to get the picture. Wacky Weekends offered a program for rich guys who needed coaching when it came to their spending habits. He glanced down at the brochure as she began turning pages. "The program starts you off with an introductory session, then you shop for new clothes."

He glanced at his jeans, which were worn to perfection. "Clothes?"

"Suits," she assured. "With your escort."

"Escort?"

"Not *that* kind of escort," she assured. "We're a reputable business."

Maybe if he kept her talking, he could figure out her exact connection to his bedmate. If worse came to worst, he could ask, but then, when a woman gave a man somebody else's name or number, it was a standard brush-off. Which meant if the real Diane knew about her friend's deception, she'd protect her.

"You'll be with the same woman all week," she was saying, pointing at a price column that made him whistle. "Again," she continued, "I know it's expensive, some would say prohibitive, but this is what you'll need to spend to impress clients and guests. After you shop and have a makeover, you'll be whisked on a week-long extravaganza.

"You'll visit art openings. Museums. Manhattan's finest restaurants. You'll go to just the sort of places where you'd be most likely to commit a faux pas." She turned another page. "Here are pictures of the truly cultured women you'll meet."

Suddenly, his hand dropped to the page. There she was! Almost as beautiful dressed in a suit as she'd been in the buff. So, she'd didn't own Wacky Weekends, but she did work here. "Who's that?"

"Uh...the escort. Signe Sargent."

"And she's available?"

Diane raised an eyebrow, looking amused. "Absolutely."

"Is she married? Uh...I wouldn't feel comfortable if..."

"Single."

"And this is all week?" He'd worked double-time during the Wildcat Certification Team testing period, so he was due vacation time.

"Yes."

"And what's the final cost?"

As she riffled through some pages, James barely noticed. He just wished he wasn't quite so relieved that Signe wasn't married. It was hard to think of her as a Signe, too; for a week, he'd been calling her Diane. He figured he'd adjust. He watched as Diane's finger stabbed the page.

He whistled at the cost.

"What do you do for a living?" she asked. "If you don't mind me asking?"

A park ranger could never afford this. He considered, then said, "I'm a mystery writer. I publish under a pseudonym." It wasn't strictly true, but he'd just dropped the first three chapters of his novel off at a publisher.

"Fantastic."

Nodding, he reached for his back pocket, then said, "I don't have my checkbook with me."

"No problem. Bring it when you come for the orientation, or we'll bill you."

"Great," he said.

And they shook on it.

SIGNE ANSWERED HER CELL on the first ring. "Hello?"

"Have I got news for you," said Diane.

Glancing apologetically at Detective Perez, who'd

called her down to Police Plaza, Signe lowered her voice and said, "This is not a good time."

"You're on for next week."

"Next week?"

"A guy came in for the Manhattan Men program, so you're definitely on the payroll. He wasn't going to sign on, but when he saw your picture, he changed his mind. He was totally wowed."

"My picture," Signe echoed. "Maybe that's a bad sign. Maybe he's an obsessive stalker or something. What if he's one of those guys who's stuck on women with short dark hair and brown eyes."

"You're getting paranoid because that detective's still questioning you—"

"As a matter of fact, that's where I am now."

"Sorry, but I thought you'd be thrilled."

She should have been. She needed the money. But ever since the weekend in the Catskills, she hadn't been able to get the park ranger off her mind. Steamy dreams awakened her nightly, and twice she'd actually gotten out of bed and taken a cold shower before dawn. She'd almost convinced herself to ask C.C. to drive her to the mountains again, or rustled up her own, unused license, so she could take herself...

"He's a hunk," insisted Diane. "And a mystery writer."

Maybe it would get her mind off her crush on a thoroughly inappropriate man. "Okay," she finally said. "I'll see you then. I've got to go."

Powering off, she lifted her gaze to the suspicious dark eyes of Alfredo Perez. He pushed the guest list from the party at the Met under her nose and read three names. "Jane Smith. Amanda Levy. Doris Jones." They were the names she'd used to get her friends into the bash. "Do you know these people?"

She blushed.

He came closer. "As I've interrogated you, I've learned one thing."

She did her best not to look guilty. "What?"

"That you're a lousy liar, Ms. Sargent." Detective Perez leaned back, rocking on his heels, and plucked an end of the handlebar mustache between his thumb and forefinger. "You want to know what I think?"

Not really. "What?"

"That you put those names on the roster so you could sneak three girlfriends into the party for the free finger food. Not to mention the million-dollar men. Now, you don't want to admit it because you didn't steal the statue. You figure I'll find it, and you'll be able to go back to work. If you admit to inviting party crashers, however, your boss won't hire you back."

He was certainly on the money. "You're the detective."

"Is that all you're going to give me?"

She hadn't felt so caught between a rock and a hard place since she'd found herself standing naked in the middle of James-the-park-ranger's cabin. Even now she could feel his hot gaze burning down every inch of her. Yes...she could almost hear his groans. He'd been so lusciously hairy and male....

"Ms. Sargent?"

Why did he have to be a park ranger? She wasn't a gold digger, but she had a clear vision of how she intended to live, and it didn't include sharing a one-bedroom cabin with a man and his cats, especially when the furniture was scarred with artwork drawn by ex-campers with pocket knives.

She blinked, realizing she'd been half wishing Diane hadn't fixed her up with a date, since she was still missing the man she'd met in the Catskills. "Excuse me, Detective Perez. Did you say something?"

He stared at her a very long moment, then he merely shook his head and said, "No. Of course not. I'm only trying to find a priceless statue, and I can tell you've got a lot on your mind. You can go now, Ms. Sargent."

5

"YOU," SIGNE WHISPERED SIMPLY.

Just as the Manhattan Men orientation was about to begin, James seated himself beside her. She felt the breath whoosh from her chest. He was just as gorgeous dressed as he'd been naked, and she should have guessed he'd favor worn jeans. The flannel shirt he'd chosen looked remarkably soft, too, and despite how stunned she was to see him—how *sorry* she was to see him, she tried to tell herself—her fingers itched to run themselves down his chest.

"You," she said again.

He looped a jeans jacket around the back of a metal fold-out chair and glanced around, taking in Diane, who was standing at the podium in front, then the other women in the room, among them Mara and C.C., who were entertaining dates.

His eyes settled on Signe again. "Me," he whispered back.

Apparently, he'd tracked her down and signed up for the workshop, and while she was flattered, she was also unsure how to handle the situation. It was just too bad that Diane hadn't recognized him from their trip to the Catskills and warned her, but of course, Diane had never seen him.

"Surprised to see me?"

"Very."

He surveyed her a long moment, seemingly not the least bit perturbed that his presence might be unwanted.

"I thought you were a park ranger," she challenged softly. "Not a mystery writer."

"And I thought you were Diane Parker-Powell."

"You caught me."

"Why'd you lie?"

She wasn't quite sure what to say. First, she'd had a crush on Gorgeous. Second, she really was under police scrutiny. Besides, this man simply didn't fit the vision she had for her life, and there was no polite way to inform him of that. "When you catch a woman in a lie, do you always follow her?"

A smile was tugging his mouth. "Most women don't lie to me."

Ah. The confident type. Knowing she should have felt more annoyed, she found herself smiling back, despite her resolve not to get involved. "How did you find me?"

"The Internet. Then I came here."

"And realized I wasn't Diane."

"Right."

"Realizing you'd been given a false name didn't discourage you?"

"Guess not."

As heat rose in her cheeks, she wished she wasn't quite so aware of the outfit she'd chosen for the evening. The tan jacket and skirt suited her, and she'd added her favorite scarf, one bursting with autumnal colors. His appreciative glance was warming her, making her feel more special than she wanted to admit, and yet she couldn't quite understand it.

He was gorgeous, yes. And yet that couldn't explain why her head felt so woozy. Both her legs felt like flowing water. Given the way she felt every time she looked at him, she could almost believe the spell had worked, or that she'd somehow taken the statue of Eros home from the Met in the backpack she sometimes carried.

Her attraction to James didn't make logical sense. Over the years, she'd had plenty of good-looking men give her attention, but none had affected her this way, not even Gorgeous Garrity. Feeling frustrated, she asked, "Why did you hunt me down?"

"You say that as if you're prey."

She offered an arched brow. "Am I?"

When he nestled back in his chair, crossing one of his well-muscled legs over the other, she wondered how such a simple gesture could make her want to drag him home and strip off all his clothes. Suddenly, she was very, very aware that her apartment was right around the corner.

"Aren't you at all happy to see me?"

"I'm not sure."

"Then you shouldn't leave things behind, Cinderella."

His voice was as enticing as she remembered. Deep and throaty, it had sounded even better when he'd been spelling out exactly where he wanted her to touch him. Pulling her mind to the issue at hand again, Signe squinted, trying to recall anything she might have left at the cabin, but she hadn't been wearing a stitch. "Cinderella left a shoe."

He squinted at her.

"I was barefoot," she reminded him.

That made him smile again, and it really was a lovely smile, one that lit up his face and made the corners of his eyes crinkle. "Naked, too."

As if she hadn't remembered. "I'm flattered that you looked me up, I really am, but..."

Pulling a ring from his pocket, he held it up. Her heart lurched. Of course, she thought. Her ring. She'd been sure she'd lost it, and she hadn't remembered wearing it to the Catskills. "You found it!"

"Beside my bed."

She couldn't help but be touched. "It was a birthday gift from my mother a few years ago. I looked everywhere for it." Truly, she'd thought she'd never see it again.

Her breath caught as he slid a palm beneath her hand. Some line she'd read years ago in college about blushing skin teased her memory. It was from Shakespeare, she thought, but she couldn't quite place it. All she knew was that time seemed to stand still when their flesh connected.

Beneath her palm, she could feel his quiver. With his other hand, he slowly slid the ring onto her finger. Only when her heart missed a beat did she realize that no man had ever done that before. She pushed away the giddy sensation, but not before imagining the two of them standing at the altar....

Whoa. Pulling herself back to reality, she realized

she really better not get into bed with him again, not with her mind running in such a direction.

She needed someone who shared her vision of life, she reminded herself, jerking her eyes away from his unflinching gaze. Statistically, people with similar backgrounds made better marriages, and she didn't want to wind up divorced. Maybe she even feared the kind of potent sexuality they'd shared. Sex had never been so...transporting.

"Really," she began again, telling herself she just felt guilty, since she knew how much Diane was charging the men who'd signed on for the program. "I'm flattered about your coming here, and being willing to pay so much to see me again, but..."

His finger silenced her. He had the audacity to raise it to her lips, and while she wasn't proud of it, it took everything she had not to suck it right into her mouth.

He whispered, "Listen up."

Diane had started talking, which was just as well. Signe needed time to collect her thoughts and restore her equilibrium. She was blown away by all this, of course. Very flattered. A park ranger had taken time off work, come down from the Catskills, lied about his occupation and paid an exorbitant price to date her for a week. Just the thought made her shivery all over.

He was all wrong for her, however, and once he had access to her naked body, she knew she'd only act as if mesmerized. Every ounce of willpower would leave her. She'd already had the requisite female fling with the woodsy adventurer. His name had been Ray Gilbert, she'd met him during her last year in college, and while his life dream had been to climb Mount Everest, he'd wound up managing a Starbucks near the Grand Canyon, to which Signe's father had snidely said, "I told you so." Her mother had defended her, chiding, "Every young woman's entitled to one mistake."

One, Signe thought now. Not two. She glanced beside her. Had she really been in bed with this hunk? Slowly, her eyes took in the large tanned hand curled over his knee, then trailed up his long-boned thigh, until her gaze settled on the bulge under his fly, where his jeans cupped him like a glove. *Abracadabra.*

He leaned closer, his lips so near to her ear that a shiver shook her shoulders. "What are you thinking?"

That you look good in clothes. "That this is not going to work out," she said. Her parents had coached her well, and they really did have her best interest and future happiness at heart, even if six feet of packed muscle coursing with testosterone had managed to turn her head again.

He changed the subject. "Why did you lie about your name? I still want to know."

Signe didn't want to interrupt her friend's presentation, but she couldn't not respond to James. "I was uncertain."

"About?"

"The possibility of seeing you again."

When Diane shot her a pointed look, Signe grabbed a pad provided with the orientation packet and jotted. "We should be quiet."

Lifting a pen from his own pocket, he wrote "Not until you tell me why you're not happy to see me."

She could barely think. His huge dark hand had pressured the pad in her lap which, in turn, had pressured her leg which, in turn, had reminded her of how good his hand had felt on that very same leg just a week before when it was bare and wrapped around his back. Now registering that he'd used a Mont Blanc pen, her eyes widened. What was a guy like him doing with such an expensive pen? Somehow, she managed to write "We'll talk afterward. Okay?"

He hesitated, then jotted back "Okay."

By the time orientation was over, Signe hoped she'd be able to nail down a graceful strategy for getting rid of him.

"I DON'T THINK IT'S A GOOD idea for me to be your escort," Signe argued an hour later in the kitchen at Wacky Weekends.

James cast a glance around a kitchen that, like all New York kitchens, was the size of a postage stamp. Which was just as well, he figured. It meant he was a scant foot from where she'd backed herself against the doorjamb, and that he was breathing in the heady, deep scents of her perfume. Since it was clean and fresh, like flowers on a spring day, he got closer. "Why not?"

"I think I've explained."

Usually, he let people have their way, especially if it came to rejecting him, not that it happened often, but this time, he wasn't buying that she really wanted rid of him. "Do you have a fiancé?"

Her lips parted. "No!"

He couldn't help but smile. "Is that so odd an idea?"

"Well, no, but..."

"You're a beautiful woman."

"Thanks, but—"

"A boyfriend?"

"No!"

"A lover?"

"No."

"I didn't qualify?"

"You're not my lover!"

He eyed her. "That's not how I recall it, Signe." Despite her protests, Signe Sargent was staring at him as if she'd like nothing more than to get back into bed with him again.

"It was just one night," she said weakly.

"And you're still looking at me as if you wouldn't mind doing it again," he returned, his voice husky.

Her breath caught. "Are you always so..."

"Bold?" he provided.

She nodded.

"No."

She almost laughed, but then caught herself and forced a stern expression. "Then why am I so honored?"

"You cast a spell." He recalled how her whimpers had rained down around his ears, stealing the very air from the room, leaving only the raw sounds of pure desire. He'd never felt that kind of a connection with a lover before. "I think you know why I looked for you, Signe."

Just gazing at her made his breath catch. She really was something to look at. Winona Ryder aside, she reminded him of Audrey Hepburn. She had the same birdlike delicacy and china-smooth skin. Her eyes were the most astonishing of her dark features. Deeply set in skin that was faintly dusky and pale, despite the hint of color left by this summer's sun, her round eyes looked like melting fudge. Dark lashes rimmed them, darker eyebrows hovered above, as perfectly arched as half moons.

"I didn't say I wasn't attracted to you."

It would have been an obvious lie. "That's a start."

Tilting her head, she seriously considered him for the first time. "You really don't take no for an answer, do you?"

Usually he did. That's why she was driving him crazy, although he wasn't about to tell her that. He wasn't the kind to let any woman turn his world upside down. "Do I have a choice?"

Relaxing against the doorjamb, she crossed her arms. "Of course. You're a free agent."

"Am I? After you cast a spell on me?"

She rolled those amazing eyes. "You don't believe that."

Trouble was, he'd sometimes wondered about it. Oh, he didn't believe in magic, and yet, before now, he'd never debased himself by not leaving at the first hint of rejection. "I'm afraid I'm starting to."

"Look," she began reasonably. "Spells don't really work. And if you're sure you're bewitched, I know a shop on West Fourth Street where they could tell you how to reverse the spell. Also, I'm not really a witch."

Could have fooled him. "You're not?"

She shook her head. "No. I just went with Diane and some friends to the Catskills, to see if the wiccan retreat could be offered as a novelty weekend."

Somehow, he was relieved that Signe wasn't really a serious practitioner of the craft. Not that the idea of white magic scared him, but somehow this demystified the crazy feelings he'd been having for her. If she wasn't really a witch, he doubted her spells would be very effective. "What exactly did you say in that spell, anyway?"

"It doesn't matter."

"It does to me. I deserve to know what I'm...a victim of."

"You're not a victim."

Sure he was. A victim of lust. "C'mon. What did you ask for?"

"Just what I told you. I hoped we'd wind up in bed. Look, it was a strange night for me. I just want you to understand. I was upset...."

He squinted. "About what?"

"Oh, a lot of things, and I drank just a bit too much...."

"How could I forget?"

"I guess what I'm trying to say is that I don't do that sort of thing usually."

As good as she was in bed, that was hard to believe. "What? Have sex?"

"Well, I have sex," she admitted. "But not with strangers."

As he edged closer, memories of what they'd done that night came fully present to him, and he had to fight not to encircle her waist with his arms and pull her against him. The second their bodies made contact, it would be all over. Her arms would wreath his neck, their hips would lock and unstoppable heat would surge.

He managed to refrain. "You're saying you wouldn't have slept with me if you hadn't been drinking?"

"No—" Her voice turned throaty, as if in reaction to his close proximity. "Not exactly, but..."

The more she looked at him, the more he realized that night had invaded her every thought, just as it had his. So, why didn't she want to see him? "Are you embarrassed because you went to a stranger's cabin?"

"I thought you were someone else."

The information hit him hard. "Someone else?"

"I thought someone I was interested in had come to the Catskills to meet me," she explained.

"In my cabin?"

"I thought it was *my* cabin."

He couldn't believe it. "You wound up in the wrong bed?"

Slowly, she nodded.

"I see." He glanced toward the main room, now anxious to gracefully back out, to go tell Diane he'd changed his mind about being included in the Manhattan Men program. "Sorry," he managed to say. "I misunderstood."

"*You* thought *I* was someone else," she pointed out.

The blond wiccan. "True, but I was in my own

bed." And he'd had every reason to believe that he'd been the man she'd wanted to make love with.

He stepped forward, meaning to pass her, his internal feelings tangled in knots...knots that tightened when she reached out her hand and grasped his elbow. Sparks seemed to skate up his arm. He felt a rush of annoyance, too. He'd come all the way to Manhattan, only to learn she'd thought he was another man. Now he wished she'd let him go. His eyes lifted from where her fingers curled on the sleeve of his shirt, then locked into hers. "What?"

"Don't..."

"Go? Isn't that what you wanted? Isn't that why you dragged me into the kitchen for this private conversation?"

"I don't understand why you're so mad. Who did you think I was?"

He shrugged. "A blond woman who stopped at the ranger's station for directions." Which was very different from what she'd thought that night, since she'd already known the man she'd thought she was sleeping with.

She was inches away now. One step, and his thigh would be between her legs. One breath, and their lips were mesh.

"Don't be angry with me," she repeated.

"You want me to leave, nice and easy? Without a scene?"

A pleading light had crept into her eyes, and when he gazed farther into the depths, he wanted to push away what he saw. The fun and games were over. The night she'd been giggling in his bed could have been a thousand years ago. He had no idea why, but everything seemed eerily charged now. The air in the kitchen seemed to turn quiet. Sounds of Manhattan—sirens and horns—seemed to recede. He felt if he'd met her before that night. In a dream. Or another lifetime. Or a parallel universe. And maybe because of that, it seemed very important not to let her go.

She whispered, "Why wouldn't you?"

Because he wanted to conquer what he was feeling. As his eyes flicked over her face, he wanted to cup her chin and trace the slightly upturned line of her lip. The shiny gloss she wore had an orange-red tint that made him think about kissing it off.

His gaze settled on the racing pulse in her throat, and he had to fight the impulse to circle his hand around her neck and stroke the soft skin. He remembered how he'd done so before, how she'd flung her head back and arched her hips, purring with need.

"Honestly," she said, unable to keep her voice from shaking, "none of this was personal."

"It's personal as hell," he found himself saying, unable to hide the thread of terseness in his voice. And then, glancing around once more, he thought he got the picture. "I'm not your type." She wanted to date the kind of guys who'd showed up for this thing, coal-mine owners and oil barrons.

"It's not that. It's just…"

His lips twisted in a wry smile. "Well, that's why I'm here, right? For a makeover? To become the kind of man you find suitable."

"It's not like that," she said miserably.

"Prove it."

"How?"

"Date a park ranger."

She looked trapped. "It just that I've wanted a particular kind of lifestyle," she tried to explain. "And I've worked hard for it."

He could imagine. "A condo in the city," he guessed. "Professional man. Gym memberships. A couple of nice clubs."

"Is something wrong with that?"

"Absolutely not," he said. And he meant it. "I'm all for choosing a lifestyle that suits your fancy."

She cocked her head, as if to better survey him, and he could tell he'd done more than pique her curiosity, even though she was trying to push him away. "Is that what you've done?"

"Yeah. And I really am writing a novel."

She was still grasping his elbow, holding it tight, as if unaware she hadn't yet let him go. Apparently, the accusation about snobbery carried some weight. "I think that sounds great," she conceded. "And you don't even know me," she murmured.

He figured he'd acquainted himself with parts of her that even some of her boyfriends hadn't. "You don't know me, either."

"Well, you are a ranger," she countered. "And I'm not very outdoorsy."

"Maybe." He smiled. "But nature likes you. You looked great drenched in lake water with leaves in your hair."

He watched color rise on her cheeks. "Thanks."

"Thank *you*."

"No need to thank me."

"True," he conceded. "Let's just chalk that whole night up to a joint effort. With nobody thanking anybody else."

"Fine by me."

They stared at each other a long moment, and once more, James wished he knew what he wanted from her. Definitely sex. And yet, he knew every kiss would only be kindling thrown on an already lit fire. It would turn into a raging inferno. She was right. He liked his bachelor's life. Given the level of attraction he felt, shouldn't he run?

He turned toward her, just slightly, but they were standing near enough that their bodies brushed. Fire doused down the front of him. He didn't bother to hold back, but pressed himself against her, just enough that she could feel his weight, his muscle. "At least tell me who he was."

"He?"

"Yeah."

Her lips were slightly parted, almost as if she was willing him to kiss her. "He who?"

Was she serious? Annoyance fused with desire as he stared down into her innocent, heart-shaped face, and he couldn't help but bring his head down until his mouth was close to hers. "The man you were crying out for in the night," he murmured huskily, the fingers that had been dangling now finding her waist. "The man you thought was in your bed, naked, waiting for you."

Her breath shallowed, and he could feel its warmth teasing his lips. Her voice was faint. "It doesn't matter who he was."

A hair couldn't have passed between their mouths now. The kiss seemed imminent, only a breath away. It felt like something he'd waited years for—not just a week. "It matters to me."

"Why?"

Because he'd thought she'd known he was the man loving her. Somehow, he couldn't stand the thought that those moans were for some unnamed rival he'd never met. When she came, convulsing around him, he'd been sure she knew he was the man sending her over the edge. "When your eyes were shut in the dark, I just want to know who you thought you were with."

Tilting her head back, she stared straight into his eyes. "You," she murmured as if entranced. "I was with you, James."

"But you didn't know it that night."

"I know it now."

He didn't want her to forget it, either. Maybe it was nothing more than his male ego. Or memories of what this woman had done for him when she'd thought he was that other man. "Do you love him?"

"No."

"You were just dating?"

"Kind of."

How could one "kind of" date? he wondered, but he let it pass. As he stared down into her eyes, all thoughts of backing out of the Manhattan Men program left him. Lowering his head that crucial fraction, he warned, "I'm going to kiss you now."

Their lips caught, fit perfectly. No air escaped. It was every bit as good as he remembered. She seemed to melt against him like a burning candle, and even though he wanted to deny it, he got the crazy feeling that he'd been away a long time and had just come home again. "Are you sure we've never met before?" he murmured.

"Yeah," she whispered.

Drawing away, he said, "I just changed my mind."

Signe looked dazed. "About?"

"I'll be needing an escort, after all." A soft chuckle came from between lips she'd just left hungry and aching. "See you tomorrow. At 8:00 a.m. sharp. Be out front." He moved to brush past her. "Oh." He turned and added, "Won't you be surprised if it turns out that I clean up nice?" he asked her.

And then he was gone.

6

"ARE YOU DECENT?" Signe stood outside a dressing room in Barney's department store.

A sexy chuckle traveled through the pulled curtain. "If I say no, will you still come in?"

Pausing, ready to lift the curtain, she couldn't help but smile. They'd been together only a few hours this morning—just long enough to have breakfast, shop for toiletries and visit a salon—and he hadn't so much as tried to kiss her yet. She was relieved, of course. At least that's what she told herself.

Nevertheless, last night, she'd been blown away to find him at Wacky Weekends. She'd gone to sleep fantasizing about his parting kiss, too, and some time before dawn had decided to meet him and have fun, just to see how things went. What could it hurt? As many warning signals as she felt, she couldn't help but be curious. All morning, she'd caught herself surreptitiously eyeing the seductive curve of his mouth. "Are you?" she repeated.

"Decent enough."

She wasn't sure what that meant, but decided to take her chances and lift the curtain. Seeing that he was dressed, she glanced over her shoulder, looking for the salesclerk before drawing the curtain farther back and entering. Because the room was cramped, not to mention round in shape, and because James was standing on a raised platform in front of three mirrors, he looked larger than usual. His body filled the whole space, as did his scent. She couldn't help but say, "That cologne smells great."

"I like it," he admitted.

They'd bought it on the ground floor, and the second Signe smelled it, she'd known it was perfect. It was one of those woodsy designer scents that evoked smoke and pine, and now she was standing close enough that she could catch hints of whatever was beneath, something difficult to define that was simply him.

Rising on her toes, she peered over one of James's broad shoulders, into the mirrors. "You were right."

He was absently surveying the suit he was wearing. "About?"

"Cleaning up nice."

"Thanks."

Earlier, they'd stopped at a salon, and while Signe now missed the overly long waves that, just yesterday, had nearly brushed the park ranger's shoulders, his new haircut made him look more sophisticated. He could pass for a man-about-town. "You could be a broker. Or a lawyer."

He laughed. "That's good?"

"Not good or bad. Just a surprise."

"Told you so."

The stylist had definitely known what he was doing. By leaving a tuft of golden bang and cutting the strands around his ears, he had made James's face more noticeable. It was quite a face, Signe thought as her eyes took in the jawline and wide strong bones beneath his eyes. Working outdoors had given his face a hint of weathered saltiness, and it had brought out lines around his eyes and mouth that made him look a little older than his years. Once he was in a suit, those same lines made him look distinguished. "The haircut's great."

He was still eyeing the suit, as if he'd never seen himself wear one, which, she figured, was possibly the case. "Really?"

She nodded. "It was a shame to hide you under all that wild hair," she coached. He might have only signed up for the Manhattan Men program to see her again, but that didn't mean Signe couldn't use the time wisely, she was deciding, to help him see how he could better use his God-given assets to the best advantage. "You've got terrific bone structure."

"Bone structure?" he echoed, as if he'd never heard the phrase.

She nodded. Raising a hand, she traced a finger along his cheek. "Very striking profile. Almost patrician. You've got a strong straight nose." She chuckled. "You could have been a Roman emperor." She paused, then added, "Except for the dimple."

"Are you sure? Didn't Julius Caesar have a dimple? And what about Nero? Or Napoleon?"

She frowned. "What? Do you sit around reading biographies of world conquerors?"

He laughed again. "Even park rangers can read, Signe."

"That's not what I meant. I—"

"And don't forget cable," he added. "Believe it or not, we do get television in the boondocks."

Putting her hands on her hips, she smirked, not about to let him make her feel like a snob. She'd done a lot of work on herself since she'd made the move to New York after attending college in Minneapolis, and even if he was resisting, she was determined to show him how glamorous he could look. "You make fun now," she warned. "But you'll like the end result. Tomorrow, you're getting a massage and facial, as well as lectures about good posture and managing stress."

"Cleaning up campsites isn't that stressful."

"Maybe." She couldn't help but chuckle. "But I recall one camper who made your blood pressure sky-rocket."

"Point taken."

"I knew you'd see my side of things."

"Maybe we should just sign me up for that television show, *Extreme Makeover*."

"You're not in that much need of help."

He laughed. "No plastic surgery?"

"Maybe a tummy tuck."

"Liposuction?"

"That, too," she said darkly.

Beneath the two-hundred-dollar shirt, his belly was as flat as a board. Right now, any of the best restaurants in the city would seat him near the front window, just to attract attention from would-be customers strolling down the sidewalk. Very definitely, the man was a diamond in the rough. Uttering a breathy sigh, Signe vaguely wondered how she could have missed the dimple beside his mouth when they'd met, but then, that morning she'd had plenty of other things on her mind.

She realized she was staring openly in appreciation. "That really does look great on you, James."

"For a suit," he conceded, looking pleased by the

compliments. His eyes met hers in the mirror. "You're saying you wouldn't be embarrassed to be seen with me, huh?"

She shot him a smile. "No."

His brows lifted, and as they did, the expression of his eyes gained depth, sparkling with humor. "You, however, will have to get one of those skimpy little black numbers. Something with no straps. Maybe a slit up the side."

"Exposed garters," she suggested, unable to resist the flirtation.

"In black."

"And no doubt the dress should be backless."

"Frontless would be better," he said, shrugging. "But I'll take backless."

"I think backless could be arranged."

"What you've got on looks nearly as good," he said, making her glad she'd chosen the dress. Pumpkin in color, its jersey fabric nearly touched her ankles, exposing just a hint of ribbed leggings and round-toed boots. A dark brown knitted shawl draped her shoulders.

Turning serious, she said, "I think I like this suit even better than the last." Although the light tan color of the first suit he'd tried had given him a more casual look that was tailored to James's personality, this was heart-stopping.

The fabric was a charcoal color the clerk had called early-morning gray. While Signe had picked a dark chocolate brown she figured would accentuate James's eyes, the clerk had insisted that they try the gray also, and now she could see that he'd been exactly right. The shirt beneath was sparkling white, with pearl studs and tiny, barely discernible gray-and-yellow stripes, and the tie the clerk had chosen showed a burst of fall colors—rust, orange and yellow.

"It doesn't even need tailoring."

"The pants need to be hemmed," he returned.

Tilting her head, she sent him a long sideways glance, to which he said, "What?"

She edged closer, and when he turned around, she slipped a finger under the tie, lifting it, enjoying the whisper of silk against her fingertips. Just as she let it drop, he said, "How's my escort feel about taking me to an Italian restaurant tonight?"

"Not in this suit." Reaching down, she caught the dangling price tag on the sleeve and showed it to him. He whistled dutifully, but she was surprised he didn't look more impressed.

He shrugged. "No problem."

She didn't believe it for a second. She'd let some men save face, but James was direct, so she could speak her mind; it was something she was quickly deciding she liked about him. "Look," she said. "I appreciate what you're doing, but..." Pausing, she wasn't exactly sure what she wanted to say, but she plunged on. "You only signed up for the Manhattan Men program because of me, James."

"True," he admitted with a chuckle. "But I think we both agree that I need something to sand off my rough edges."

"Well," she conceded, thinking what a good time she'd had so far, especially since James was getting her mind off her problems with Detective Perez. Funnier still, ever since she'd met James, Gorgeous had simply vanished from her awareness, as if she'd never even had a crush on him in the first place. If she didn't know better, she'd think she'd truly cast the spell on James, not Gorgeous.

Pushing away the thoughts, she said, "Maybe it's okay to spend time together, and the cost of everything, except the clothes and dinner checks, is included in the program fee." Pausing, she frowned. "I insist that you don't buy the suits, though, and as far as the meals are concerned, we'll go Dutch."

"Otherwise, you're going to teach me how to walk and talk like a gentleman?" he concluded, his voice lilting as he paraphrased words from *My Fair Lady*.

"I just love that musical."

"You like musicals?"

"Especially that one."

"Let's put a Broadway show on the agenda."

"Really?"

"If you think you can trust me to mind my p's and q's."

"Given the morning we've spent together, you're much better mannered than I would have imagined," she admitted.

His eyes sparkled with devilment. "Well, Signe," he reminded, "you haven't really had a lot of experience being around me, you know. Maybe you've made some snap judgments."

How he'd acted in bed probably wasn't a very strong indicator of how he'd act while ordering dinner in a restaurant, she silently conceded. "Maybe," she admitted. Still, she didn't want a hard-working park ranger to buy a suit from Barney's just to impress her. "The thing is," she said, "you're never going to wear this suit."

"I thought we were going to dinner tonight."

"We don't have to go where we're expected to dress."

"What if I *want* to go where we're expected to dress?" he countered.

She gulped around a lump that was mysteriously forming in her throat. Dressing up and sharing dinner with a man who looked this good was immensely appealing. He really seemed to like her, too. While he might not match the dream image she'd always had in her mind about her future mate, he was shaping up to be fun. However, unlike the other men in the program, such as the coal miner and the oil man, James really couldn't afford this. "I've seen your cabin," she pointed out.

Still looking totally nonplussed, he simply grinned at her. "And?"

She squinted at him playfully. Despite her intention last night to insist they not go through with his makeover this week, she was actually enjoying his company and the banter. "I recall scarred furniture. Two mangy cats. And a closet full of flannel shirts."

"Which means I'm due to get a suit."

"To wear to?"

"My own funeral."

She smirked. "Which takes place when?"

"After you don't sleep with me again and I kill myself."

"Not funny."

"Okay. Other people's funerals," he amended with

a laugh. "Maybe even weddings. And then, like I said, to dinner with you. Let's not forget that."

She gave up arguing. It was no use. "Well, you don't have to buy it," she said.

He merely smiled. "I love making you feel guilty."

"I don't feel guilty," she defended, vaguely perturbed to find that he'd so easily keyed into her emotional structure and what made her tick.

"Sure you do." His arm slid around her waist, and as he pulled her closer to him, ripples rushed through her whole system. "You're thinking I'm buying this suit, one I'll never wear again, just to impress you," he said. "And you think I feel railroaded somehow, as if I have to do it, because otherwise you'll think I really am a rube from the backwaters."

That was about the size of it, not that Signe was really thinking clearly any longer. Her fingers settled on his sleeves and slowly skated upward, toward his shoulders, where they finally came to rest. His eyes were piercing, looking so deeply into hers that she felt positively giddy. He had such expressive eyes, she thought.

"I appreciate all your concern, Signe, but I want you to know one thing."

"What?"

"I promise, I never do what I don't want to do."

"No wonder you were so worried about my casting a spell on you then," she teased.

"Maybe when it comes to you," he returned, "your spell and my thinking aren't exactly at odds. I've been thinking about you and me...."

She'd been thinking about it, too. There was no denying it, and ever since the kiss last night, she'd wanted another. "I know," she managed to say. "But I really meant what I said. I don't want to get involved right now."

"I was thinking about getting into bed, not getting involved."

Maybe. But he was willing to buy a suit with an exorbitant price tag, just to wear to dinner with her. As good as he looked in it, it was clear that he loved the life he'd built for himself in the mountains. "Look," she said. "You love your life."

"True."

"And the fact is—" She raised a staying hand. "Just being in your cabin kind of gave me the willies." Even if she went in with a mop and broom, and gave it a thorough scrubbing, she'd never be comfortable there.

"We should go to your place instead," he suggested reasonably. "At the moment it's a lot closer than the Catskills."

"James," she countered. "You were willing to sign on for a Manhattan Men program that you didn't really need, and now you're talking about buying a suit you'll never wear, just so we can go out to dinner for one night, and for me, to be perfectly honest, this sends up warning flags." There. She'd said it. She certainly didn't want him changing his ways for her, especially after a one-night stand.

Angling his head, he lowered it so much that she was sure he was about to kiss her. "Signe," he murmured. "I think you're taking all this far too seriously."

She squinted at him, unable to refrain from pressing her body closer. "Seriously?"

"Yeah. I mean, you're absolutely right. I love my life."

"I know." All during breakfast, he'd regaled her with tales about things in which she'd never have guessed she could be so interested: his wildcat-capture team certification test, for instance, and how he'd rescued the cats she'd seen in his cabin. Although he was the black sheep in his family, he still had family ties and was staying with a brother in the city.

"Which is one reason I'm a confirmed bachelor."

This was getting interesting. "How confirmed?"

"Very."

"Why?"

"I don't trust women."

"Burned in the past?"

"Who hasn't been? And it sounds as if you want to marry, but preferably someone professional. Remember when I said I was a black sheep? It's mostly because nobody thinks I'll ever settle down. My aunt Anna has actually cut me out of her will, I think." Not looking the least upset, he laughed. "I failed every expectation. Wrong schools," he said. "Wrong hobbies." Lowering his voice, so his words were infused with dark menace, he added, "Wrong women."

Her lips twitched with amusement. "Wrong in what way?"

His eyes lasered into hers. "Oh, you know," he teased. "Skirts too short. Tops too tight."

"Sounds dangerous."

Slowly, he shook his head. "Fun," he corrected her. Suddenly aware of the pulse in her throat, she

sucked in a sharp breath trying to steady it. "I'm all
for fun." Oh, God, what was she saying?

"Do you think we could just have sex, Signe?"

She knew better, but she simply couldn't help herself. "And not make it complicated?"

"Yeah."

The man was brilliant, she suddenly thought.
Blessed with such common sense. Her mind *had* run
ridiculously wild, hadn't it? She'd been worrying
about his buying suits, and whether his inclusion in
the Manhattan Men program was good for his bank
balance. "I don't know what came over me," she
apologized, realizing she'd just been afraid he was
getting too serious about her, too fast.

"Consider me the kind of guy a woman has a casual fling with."

What if her heart got in the way? "And then?"

"Go marry your stockbroker."

"Your lips to God's ears." Call her finicky, but
she'd worked hard, keeping up her grades and wai-
tressing, studying and hoping that would help her
land her dream job at the Met; she'd even lived with
five roommates her first year in the city.

Now that James had put his cards on the table, so to
speak, she felt relieved for the first time since last
night. The way he'd tracked her down really had
made her nervous, and yet, he'd totally replaced Gorgeous Garrity as the star of her dreams. "My apartment's downtown," she found herself saying. "In the
Village."

His voice was thick with promise. "Let's take a cab.
There's plenty out front."

"Why are we still standing here?"

"Because you're considering kissing me first, before we hail the taxi."

Her soft chuckle took her by surprise. "Is that what I'm doing?"

Just as he nodded, the clerk's voice sounded. "Can I get you two anything?"

What Signe wanted, she already had. James was in her arms, and in a few moments, he'd be in her bed. Those hazel eyes were still on hers.

James lifted his voice. "We've found everything we need."

"Everything's all right then, sir?"

Without breaking the gaze, James said, "The suits are great. We'll take both of them." And then, lowering his voice so only she could hear, he whispered, "Everything's more than all right."

"This is it," she said, glancing around and wondering if he'd like what she'd done with the place, and hoping that the focus on the apartment might take the edge off how she was feeling. All the way downtown, he'd held her hand in the back seat of the cab. Her heart had been hammering, and even though she could barely believe it, her thighs were quivering in anticipation of being in bed with him again.

He whistled. "Pretty swank."

"Two bedrooms," she said proudly, fighting, but being unable to conceal, the excited hitch in her voice as she watched him take in her pride and joy, the fireplace.

"Finding so much space on this block is difficult," he said, squinting at her. "Much less something affordable."

"How do you know so much about Manhattan real estate?"

"The Catskills aren't exactly on another planet."

True. And he had said his brother lived in the city. "My girlfriend, C.C.'s, a real estate agent," she continued. "And it's a five-year legal sublet. I got it for a gazillion dollars under market value."

"That explains it."

As he glanced through the floor-to-ceiling living room windows, which were covered by ornate wrought-iron bars, she said, "My girlfriends helped me decorate."

He looked impressed. "You could go into business as interior designers."

"Thanks." He wasn't the first to say so. In the room, red predominated. Old wicker furniture had been painted, and a black carpet covered the floor. Brightly colored knickknacks from street fairs stood on shelves, and a tall red Mexican pot held a spray of dried flowers that C.C. had arranged. The sofa was arrayed with oddly shaped throw pillows made by Mara, who sewed in her spare time.

Diane had come up with the idea of collecting sheer curtains from secondhand stores, all in strong, vibrant colors—rose-reds, emerald-greens, royal-blues and sunny-yellows. After they'd collected reams of fabric, the women had sewn the tops of the curtains together, so that light shined through layer after layer of airy multi-colored magic. Looped over the bamboo sticks serving as curtain rods, a valance had been fashioned of red silk.

Admiring the window treatments, James said, "They look like they belong in a harem, somehow."

She laughed. "Have you been in many harems lately?"

"Not lately. But I'm always game."

"Consider this your first." Her smile tempered and she stared around, suddenly forlorn. "The lease is up in two years."

Sending another look around the high-ceilinged room, he said, "That could be a little depressing. Steals like this are hard to come by." He added, "But do me a favor and don't go the *Slaves of New York* route."

She thought of the story about people staying with their partners in New York, just because the rents were so high. "You read the book?"

"Saw the movie."

Practically every time the man opened his mouth, he surprised her again. He seemed to genuinely appreciate her and her girlfriends' decorating talents, which was more than she could say for many of her dates, and even better, he watched romantic comedies. Or, at least, he'd watched one. "You like movies?"

"Love them."

"Really?"

His eyes were sparkling. "Sure. There's not much to do in my cave, but I do have a Blockbuster in town. The cats and I eat popcorn together."

Realizing her eyes had drifted downward, over his worn jeans, she quickly glanced upward. "I like movies, too."

"I knew we'd have something in common, if we just looked hard enough."

"Everybody in America likes movies," she countered.

"Do you always push men away?"

She couldn't help but return his smile. "Only when I'm about to sleep with them."

His eyes were hot on hers again. Fires burned in the depths. "Maybe we should quit wasting our time, then, Signe."

"Why don't you look around at the rest of the place," she suggested. "I'll get us something to drink."

"Fine by me."

She was literally shuddering as she watched him recede into the shadows of her hallway, heading exactly where she'd meant him to—her bedroom. Turning on her heel, she pushed through double Dutch doors into the kitchen, hoping she still had the bottle of bubbly C.C. had given her on her last birthday. It was worth a king's ransom, and C.C. had sworn the stuff, which she'd tried while on a date with somebody in high finance, had tasted like liquid gold. If memory served Signe correctly, she and her friends had talked about drinking the bottle the night Mara had broken up with Dean, but then, at the last minute, they'd gone around the corner to Gus's instead.

"Yes!" she whispered, pulling the prize bottle from its hiding place in the refrigerator, behind a thick grouping of condiment bottles. Within seconds, she'd opened it, her heart beating faster with every movement. What was he doing? she wondered as she fished around in a cabinet, now looking for the champagne flutes Diane had given her two Christmases ago. Had he found the bed yet?

She hoped he was as impressed with the decor in the bedroom. Last year, she'd treated herself to a white iron bed with posts that nearly reached the ceiling. Everything else was white, feminine and frilly. While men wouldn't want to live in such a room, most who'd seen it found it incredibly sexy. It was just girlie enough that it could make a man feel like a man.

Finally finding the champagne flutes, Signe lifted them to the light, checked for spots, then slipped the stems through her fingers. "All set."

Taking a deep breath, she headed for the bedroom.

"He found it all right," she murmured a moment later, stopping across the threshold and staring at the bed. *Tell me no.*

James had gotten under the covers, pulled them to his chin, and now he was snoring. How could a man fall asleep in just five minutes? As Signe watched the covers rise and fall, his massive chest lifting them as he breathed, she felt herself deflate. So much for the wild sex she'd been anticipating. Warring emotions claimed her. First she felt more maternal than she'd have imagined possible. No doubt he was tired, after coming down from the Catskills just to see her, which meant she should let him sleep.

On the other hand, she'd just opened the bottle of her best bubbly, and if he didn't wake up, it was going to get flat. And anyway, she'd expected him to be wide awake. Waiting. Having turned down the bed. Maybe even naked. She'd even secretly hoped he'd rifled around in her bedside drawer and stacked up a few condoms.

But no. He was lying flat on his back, his hands

clasped under the covers, across his chest. Sighing, she muttered a soft "drat," then set the bubbly on a dresser, along with the two glasses, put her hands on her hips and stared at him, as if that would somehow change the situation.

She was still contemplating her next move when one of James's hands moved, grasping a corner of the covers, then his eyes opened. A smile tugged the corners of her mouth. He hadn't been asleep, after all. In fact, the man looked very awake. His lips stretched wider until they attained a full, tantalizing grin, his teeth as sparkling white as the covers he lay beneath.

And those eyes! They really were something. Signe was sure no man had ever looked at her in quite this way. Forcing herself to breathe, she managed not to glance away, intending to hold that sexy gaze just as long as he thought he could stand it.

His eyes moved first. She could almost swear he was disrobing her with nothing more than that look. She'd left her shawl in the living room. And now, the rest of her clothes seemed to be melting away from her body—as if the buttons of her pumpkin dress were magically undoing themselves, and as if the stockings were simply loosening, rolling down her legs until they puddled near boots that were walking away from her feet, moving of their own accord.

Deciding she could make her own magic, Signe reached for the buttons. One by one, she slipped a manicured finger beneath them and was startled to find how easily they opened, as if what she'd just imagined was really true—she was undressing by magic. The sides of the dress fell away. She wore no slip. Just a white push-up bra, so low cut it exposed the pink nipples she knew he could see through the lace. The thick waistband to a pair of matching lace French-cut panties nestled just beneath something else that made his eyes widen—a thin silver hoop in her navel that she hadn't worn to the Catskills.

"Any tattoos?" he asked huskily.

"No. But maybe you can draw some on."

"I'd be obliged. Do you have any pictures in mind?"

"Besides a heart with your name in it, sweetheart?" she joked in her best come-hither-sailor voice. "Not a thing."

When she shrugged out of the dress, he said in a tone so lazy it coiled into her blood like a silken ribbon that had just caught fire, "Very nice."

"Glad you approve."

"And yet everything has room for improvement."

"Such as?"

"I'd like you much better if you were over here, Signe."

"Just wait, my pretty."

"If you don't hurry," he promised, "I'm coming to get you."

"I brought us a little bubbly," she returned, reaching beside her to pour a glass, deciding they could share it, her mouth dry, her voice hoarse. Tilting back the flute, she wetted her lips, the effervescent bubbles teasing her tongue. And then she took a step toward the bed, a giggle sounding. "I really did think you were asleep, James."

"Fooled you," he murmured.

And then he pulled back the covers.

He'd been naked under the covers, too. And every

bit as gorgeous as he'd looked that morning in the cabin. "You certainly did," she managed, her eyes trailing down every inch of a rock-hard body honed by hours of working outdoors under a hot summer sun.

With one more deep, enervating breath, she circled the bedside and handed him the flute. "Drink up," she suggested as she released the front catch of her bra. "Because you're going to need it."

But James didn't move. Instead, he waited until she was lying naked beside him. And then, very slowly, he poured the bubbly onto her bare skin, dribbling it from her collarbone, between her breasts, and all the way down her belly, not stopping until the last drop had nestled in her feminine curls.

And *then* he began to drink up.

7

JAMES TRIED TO CONCENTRATE on what Signe was saying, but it was difficult, since he was sure somebody was following them. Half listening, he glanced over his shoulder as they made their way farther up the circular ramp at the Guggenheim Museum, which was exhibiting a group of paintings by a new SoHo artist, Ralph Klein, whose specialty was cat portraiture. Given James's interest in the animals, Signe had felt this might be the best way to introduce him to museum etiquette.

Now James bristled. Sure enough. The guy was about twenty paces back, trying to fade into the woodwork. As if he could. In a cheap blue suit and mustard-splattered tie, the man looked thoroughly out of place in the well-heeled crowd.

"I just love this one," Signe was saying breathlessly, pausing before a portrait. "It's of two Bengal kittens. Isn't what Klein's doing brilliant? Just compare this to the portrait of the Egyptian Mau we just saw. Or the Cornish Rex. The cats are the perfect medium to show what the man can do with a brush. The detail is phenomenal. I mean, the pictures are all delightful, and cats always have such undeniable personality, but he really makes them come to life. Don't they look real?"

James had to admit that he could almost feel the softness of the fur. He pointed. "I like the black one."

She chuckled, taking in a picture of a black kitten, with its back arched and hair raised, standing against a backdrop of Halloween items, among them a jack-o'-lantern, witch's hat and broomstick.

"One of your broomsticks?" he asked.

She shrugged. "No. But that might be my bell, book and candle."

He chuckled. "I love that old Jimmy Stewart movie." He eyed her. "Are you sure that's not bell, book and scandal, though?"

"Scandal?"

"A woman like you could easily embroil a man in one."

"You give me way too much credit."

He shrugged, considering the cats again. "They're the strangest-looking felines I've ever seen."

"That's because they're pedigreed."

James could only shake his head. "They really breed cats that look like tigers?"

"Bengals like these? Sure. The Bengal breed was the result of an experimental mating between a domestic female shorthair and an Asian leopard cat in the 1960s. Aren't they cute? They actually look like kitten-size tigers. I've always wanted one."

"They have the same markings."

"I really like the Devon Rex, too."

Curling his fingers more tightly around Signe's elbow, he drew her closer as he cast a glance at the guy behind them. Maybe it was his imagination, but he was sure the man was following them. "Those are the cats with really curly hair, right?"

"Right. You don't see many of them. Other breeds, such as Persians, Siamese and Abyssinians are more well known."

"I kind of like my mutts," remarked James, wondering what the guy was up to, and vaguely hoping the cats were fine. He'd dropped them off at the animal-rescue center for the week. "I'm against anything pedigreed."

"And you think *I'm* a snob?"

He shook his head. "Believe me, you can do no wrong." He cast another glance at the picture she'd been viewing. "As for the Bengal kittens, I admit I'd make an exception."

She flashed him a glorious smile that made his chest grow tight. For the past three days, he'd nearly moved into her apartment. He was still changing clothes at his brother's place, but that was about it. So far, the sex was stellar. Absolutely amazing. They accommodated each other as if they'd been making love together for years, and yet nothing seemed rote or scripted. They'd shared deeply, too, not holding back emotion, and that had been a new experience for him.

At night, they'd taken to strolling the city, window-shopping and people watching, and they'd gone to the Broadway show they'd discussed, as well as the Italian dinner. They'd also covered all the New York must-dos, including the lobbies of famous hotels and landmark buildings. For him, the trip to Ground Zero had been the most affecting. He'd watched as her eyes had grown misty, and she'd told him where she'd been that day, and about the volunteer work she and her girlfriends had done in the aftermath.

Given what they'd shared, James felt as if he'd known Signe for years, not just days. Ever since the first night in the cabin, he'd had the strangest feeling about being with her, as if knowing her was, somehow, preordained. Destined by the stars. Fated.

He really didn't know what to make of it. And no matter what it meant, he told himself, he definitely wasn't the marrying kind. Still, he was beginning to think he wanted...a relationship. No other woman had ever affected him like this.

He realized the guy was still behind them. No. He wasn't wrong. He was definitely following them, and he had his eye on Signe. Had he seen her outside and decided to follow her in? She was attractive enough to pique the interest of a stalker. Especially today. In a rust-colored suede blazer over black pants that flared over trendy zippered black boots, she looked very chic.

He turned to Signe again. She was saying, "Look closely at the detail in this picture. Isn't it something? Before Klein found success with the cat portraits, he followed a path very similar to Andy Warhol's. He graduated from the Pittsburgh Art Institute, then worked as an illustrator of children's books."

James slowed his steps, since they were reaching the top of the walkway, deciding to let the man catch up with them. Ahead was a series of wall partitions, just large enough that a single painting could hang from them. Squinting, he used the glass covering a framed photograph as a mirror, keeping his eyes on his quarry as he continued. "How do you know all this stuff?"

"I studied art in college," she said, stopping in front of another painting. "It's my passion. And Klein really is wonderful. A few months ago, I went to hear him speak in an art forum at Columbia. Some of the cats were there."

Sure enough, as James stilled his steps, the man ducked around the other side of the partition. Out of the corner of his eye, James watched the man approach. He definitely had nerve. Was he really going to stand on the other side of the partition, opposite James and Signe, and eavesdrop on their conversation?

"In his presentation," Signe was saying, "Klein talked about how he mixed the gold for the eyes of this British Blue. He mixes all his own paints, but this color is really astonishing. It's so rich and soft. Almost like velvet. Don't you think so, James?"

He barely heard. He was too busy reaching around the side of the partition. Just as his hand closed over the sleeve of the man's sport coat, he yanked, and the man staggered out. He wasn't much to look at. Pencil thin, he was wearing the most ludicrous handlebar mustache James had ever seen. Surely, it was a fake. But no...it was the real thing.

James's eyes fixed on the other man, and just in case he intended to run, he tightened his grip until his fingers fisted around a sleeve. Keeping his voice calm and his gaze level, he demanded, "Who are you?"

The man stared back stoically. "I think Ms. Sargent

knows," he said. And then he reached into his back pocket, brought out a wallet of black cracked leather and flipped it open to expose a gold shield.

"His name's Detective Perez," explained Signe moments later, as she seated herself on the ledge of a large enclosed flowerbed outside the Guggenheim. As James slid next to her, she tried to tamp down her anger. Leave it to Detective Perez to ruin a perfectly lovely afternoon. Emotions were coursing through her that she couldn't begin to piece apart. Everything inside was tangling into knots. She simply couldn't believe the man was following her, especially when she was with a date. This meant Perez knew exactly who her best friends were by now, and he'd probably matched them to the still pictures from the security camera at the Met.

Her heart was still beating double time from the confrontation inside. Not much had happened, really. Perez had just flipped his badge out for the world to see as if Signe was the world's worst criminal. She sent James a sideways glance. How much should she tell him? He was hunched over, his shoulders hunkered down as if he was trying to make himself shorter, just so that he could better look into her eyes. He was worried, and trying to make sure she was okay. In fact, he looked so sincerely concerned that guilt coursed through her. After all, she had lied to the police, hadn't she? Or at least omitted part of the truth.

"So you weren't lying about the stolen statue?" he probed.

She shook her head. "No," she admitted. What I said that morning in the cabin was true. You see, I've wanted to work at the Met ever since I can remember. Which is why I studied art in college and library science."

He frowned. "But you were working at the café?"

She'd told him that much as they'd come outside. She nodded. "Yeah. I'd been applying for some time while I was working for the New York Public Library, and I thought if I switched to the Met, even in reduced circumstances, so to speak, that I'd get to know some of the people on staff...." Her voice trailed off. So much for best-laid plans.

"Good strategy. You'd be very good," he said kindly. "You have degrees and you know a lot about art."

He was just being nice, she thought, tears stinging her eyes. After all, a park ranger could hardly evaluate her job skills in fine arts. His trying to do so was so remarkably sweet that she reached out a hand, closed it over his strong forearm, squeezed and said, "Thanks, James."

"No need to thank me. You clearly know what you're doing."

Maybe so. She knew a lot about art history, at any rate. "I have an advanced degree in library science." But right now, it seemed that all her hard-won education would wind up going to waste. Taking a deep breath, she plunged into the story about the Halloween party, even though she'd already given him bits and pieces on their way outside. "The party was given by a computer mogul, a friend of one of the

Garritys," she explained. "I don't know if you've heard of them, but they're a wealthy family." Pushing aside recollections of the way Gorgeous had flirted with her despite his upcoming marriage, she added, "Very old money."

He was silent a long moment. "Uh-huh."

"They own a lot of artwork," she plunged on. "Some of the pieces in the Met are on loan from family members." Pausing, she shook her head slowly, exhaling in a low wolf's whistle. "Can you imagine?" she asked. "Actually owning a Rembrandt or a Vermeer? Having a Degas right in your living room?"

When she glanced at him for confirmation, he looked uncertain about what to say and she hardly blamed him. Money such as the Garritys was difficult for average people such as them to contemplate. "Anyway," she continued, blowing out another sigh, "the night of the party, Harold Garrity—he's the one married to Anna Garrity, who was previously a Marmaduke, and who was rumored to have almost married Hans Johannes, the tennis pro—"

"I can see you really are one for history."

She drew a deep breath. "I am. I like to read the society page." She shot him a long glance. "But I am not a gold digger."

His lips quirked. "Sure you are. But you're only trolling for a middle-class professional. Not the big cheese."

She was surprised to feel her own smile broadening. The man really did have a sense of humor. "You can't blame me for wanting a nice lifestyle."

James shrugged philosophically, his eyes turning liquid with mock sorrow. "What about *amour?*"

"Who ever said that love and a nice lifestyle should be mutually exclusive?"

"Touché."

"Anyway, as I was saying," she continued, returning to the earlier topic. "That night, the statue Harold Garrity loaned to the museum was stolen. It's a nameless fetish, often called Eros of the Nile, and it's reputed to bring sexual potency." Suddenly, she shuddered and wrapped her arms around herself.

He squinted. "You okay?"

"Fine. Just cold." The last vestiges of Indian summer were gone for good. Sighing deeply, she glanced up and found herself looking into a tree planted in the sidewalk. The pruned branches were nearly bare. For a second, all thoughts left her except that winter was coming, and that she'd love to have someone to spend it with, curled before the fireplace in her apartment, watching the flames lick the logs and turn to burning hot embers. Her eyes trailed down to the concrete, where the fallen leaves, which had been so vibrant in rusts, reds and golds were curling and becoming brittle. Even the pavement was getting that winter look—turning darker and strangely mottled. Daylight savings time had just begun, and although it was only afternoon, night seemed to be approaching.

"Here," James murmured, stretching an arm around her back and pulling her close. Being drawn into the embrace felt like magic. As she sighed and melted against his chest, pressing her cheek against his jeans jacket, the smell of pine filled her lungs. Briefly, she shut her eyes. "You feel good."

He squeezed her more tightly. "Good. I'm glad."

She blew out a sigh. "You know," she murmured, leaning back a fraction, just enough that she could gaze up into his eyes. "I could use a cup of coffee."

"Wait here."

He gave another quick, reassuring squeeze, then stood, saying, "Be right back, doll."

She registered the moment his eyes landed on an outdoor kiosk farther up Fifth Avenue, then she watched as he darted through traffic, heading toward it. What a nice guy, she couldn't help but think, her heart swelling as she watched him vanish through the door. He'd protected her from Detective Perez, and now he was getting coffee. She took another deep breath, tears misting her eyes again.

Every once in a while, in life, she thought, somebody happened to make the exact right small gesture at the exact right moment. James's going for coffee was such an event. Already, she could feel the warmth and taste the smooth, reassuring brew. It was as if just a sip would fix all her problems. It wouldn't, but it sure felt that way. She couldn't wait for him to get back to the museum, sit beside her and hug her.

Just a couple of minutes later, he came toward her again, looking luscious and carrying two coffees, his jacket flapping open in the breeze, exposing a red-white-and-blue flannel shirt that looked oddly out of place on the Upper East Side and made her lips tug into another smile.

When he was close enough to hear, she said, "Did

anyone ever tell you that you look like a lumber-jack?"

In a put-on country accent, he said, "As cold as it's getting, darlin', maybe I should saw us some logs and build a fire."

Maybe the whole outdoor mystique wasn't as much of a negative as she'd initially assumed. "Exactly what I was thinking. Sounds nice."

He sat beside her. "A little cider. A big fur rug."

She sent him a mock frown. "I thought you were an animal rights activist. You know, given that you've got a Wildcat Capture Team certification card."

His eyes twinkling, he said, "I already caught the wildcat I was after."

Her lips twitched. "I'm serious."

"Okay. Faux fur," he amended.

"Good. Otherwise someone might bomb us with red paint."

"Are they still doing that to people who wear fur in the city?"

"Who knows?" She glanced down at her suede coat. "I confess to being a leather girl."

"You'd think leather would cause the same ruckus."

She shrugged, realizing how much she did enjoy bantering with him. Conversation just seemed to flow. There were no long awkward silences. No major disagreements about life, and how it should be lived, despite her professed desire to have a lifestyle different from his. "I guess there's no logic when it comes to justice," she offered.

"Here," he said.

He pulled back the tab on her coffee cup lid, blew inside, then handed her the coffee. It was good coffee, too. Rich and dark, with just the right amount of cream. She couldn't help but be reminded of a man she'd dated last year named Steven Stuart. After three months, he still couldn't remember how she took her coffee, and that had been the reason she'd broken up. As usual, her father had said, "I told you so," and her mother had agreed. If a man couldn't remember how you took your coffee, her mother had argued, how could he remember anything of deeper consequence? Signe took a deep draught and let the hot liquid warm her through. As James did the same, he wrapped his free arm around her back once more, pulling her closer to his side. Nobody's hug had ever felt as right as his at that moment.

"Why does Detective Perez think you took the statue?"

"It was my job to turn on the alarms."

"And you did."

Her heart swelled. He was the first person, other than her girlfriends, to give her the benefit of the doubt. Her parents would have, of course, but she couldn't bring herself to tell them about the theft, or that she'd lost her job. "Yes. He doesn't believe me, but I know I did. I can almost see myself doing it. I know I didn't screw up."

"Did you see anything suspicious?"

She shook her head. I've been over it all a million times. Both with the police and in my own mind. I think Detective Perez questioned everyone." She frowned. "The only people he might have bypassed were the kids who were there."

"Kids?"

She nodded. "Yeah. There were a bunch. The party was a Halloween bash, like I said, and it was held in the Temple of Dendur," she continued. "There were a lot of people there that night, and a number of them brought their kids."

A smile glimmered on her lips. "They were cute, too. Dressed up in the usual costumes. One was a pumpkin, I remember. And one little girl was the most adorable witch...." Her voice trailing off, she shrugged.

"You like kids, huh?"

"Who doesn't?"

"They are fun."

"Can't argue with that," she said, trying to ignore that topics usually associated with serious dating were starting to creep into their conversations, such as whether or not they liked kids, and how they felt about politics. "Anyway, I know how thorough Detective Perez has been with me, so I'm sure he's researched every possibility."

Her throat tightened. "I was doing so well. I was working hard."

He sounded surprised. "You say that as if you usually don't."

She considered. "Not true. But I'm an only child, and younger than most of my friends, probably because I've always been used to being around older people. What I'm trying to do now is..." Hesitating, she shrugged. "Make it on my own. Do something for myself. I want that job so badly. I'd made friends in the archives department where I wanted to work, and I know I'd be perfect for the job. I could really use what I know. I can't lose that opportunity. And I can't work for Diane forever."

"You'd get to date sexy men like me," he pointed out.

"No offense, but I have other life dreams."

"Now, don't get self-pitying on me."

"Sorry."

"Don't be sorry, either."

She couldn't help but laugh. "What can I do?"

He winked. "I'm sure I can think of something."

She sighed, taking another sip of her coffee. "I just thought all this would be cleared up by now. My boss, Edmond Styles...well, I know he really wanted to hire me. The night the statue was stolen, he told me that one of the women in archives was ready to give notice and the job would be mine. I haven't had the nerve to call and see if he filled the position with somebody else.

"Well, for the moment, I've got an idea," said James.

She squinted. "What?"

"When I watched the movie *Serendipity*, I noticed the soda parlor by that name. I mean, when women are depressed, that movie seemed to suggest that they like to gorge—"

"On chocolate?" she finished.

"So it seems. So, I was thinking we might head to Serendipity and share a really gooey, expensive, decadent banana split."

"Awesome," she whispered, staring up at him. "You're almost as cool as my girlfriends."

"Almost?"

She shrugged. "Sorry, but I've known them longer. And...well, face it. Girlfriends are kind of like pets."

"How so?"

"After the men leave, the girlfriends are always still there."

"Maybe," he conceded. "But I can do a few things your girlfriends can't."

"Such as?"

"I'll show you that," James promised, "right *after* we go to Serendipity."

SIGNE LEANED HER HEAD BACK two hours later, further exposing her neck as she sucked a deep, shivery breath between her teeth, barely able to believe how adventurous this man was. Through half-shut eyes, she could see the flickering flames in the fireplace. On the way back to her apartment, James had insisted on stopping at a deli for hot cider and mulling spices as well as a bouquet of flowers, which now sat by the fireplace, and wood, with which he'd built the first fire of the season. Climbing toward ecstasy, she melted now as he squeezed a squirt bottle and swirled hot, runny chocolate around and around her breast, narrowing the spiraling circle until he reached a taut tip. Blowing out a shaky breath, he didn't stop until the nipple was thoroughly coated.

His voice husky, he said, "It's a good thing we could buy this chocolate to go."

"If we'd done this in Serendipity," she murmured

in agreement, excitement catching in the back of her throat, "we'd have been arrested, James."

Leaning, he angled his head down, and as he did, the silken tips of his hair brushed her cheek, feeling like heaven. His lips brushed hers, settled and drank, and then they moved on. When they found the tail end of the chocolate maze he'd drawn, a low moan emanated from deep in her chest. Somehow, she'd hoped he'd start where she wanted to feel him most, where her nipple was bathed in the gooey confection.

No such luck. She should have known James better than that by now. He meant to torture her. The pointed spear of his tongue felt damp and lusciously cool against the heated surface of skin warmed by his caresses and the fire. Prickles washed over her as his tongue wiggled, teasing her. He was good, she thought. Oh, so good. That pointed spear was pure magic, eating up the line of chocolate he'd drawn on her body ever so slowly....

"Take your time," she whispered.

"I am," he whispered back.

Already, he'd plied her body with his hands—exploring the soft arches of her feet, the sweet backs of her knees, the rounded curves of her hips. Splaying a hand on her belly, he'd simply let it lie there, until she was hungry with want for his touch. And then, as if sensing when her need reached its peak, he'd begun to move the hand, massaging both breasts, kneading them leisurely, as if they had until the end of time. He'd stroked the sides, using nothing more than the backs of his fingers....

Now, between licks, he said, "Detective Perez wants to arrest you, anyway."

"I'm not afraid," she murmured, her already taut nipples now more painfully tight, begging silently for the onslaught of his mouth, the moment when those firm, hot lips that kept kissing her senseless would latch on to one of them. His tongue would bathe her then. She'd be wet all over. He'd draw her deep between his lips, suckling hard, spilling liquid across her chest. She shifted on the blanket, moisture dampening the silk of the panties she suddenly wished she wasn't wearing.

His tongue was still swirling in the chocolate. He was going oh-so-slow. Licking here, licking there—but never quite managing to touch that stiffened nipple. She whimpered. Twisted her hips.

After a long moment, he murmured, "You're not?"

Her mind reached, but she could no longer remember what they'd been talking about. She wasn't sure what was hotter, her skin or the panties, but she wanted every last stitch of her clothes gone. Vaguely, as his tongue continued its maddening trail, she said, "Huh?"

"Afraid," he reminded.

Oh, right. They'd been talking about Detective Perez. "Nope," she managed to say, her voice shaky, her breath shallow. "I have perfect faith that you'll break me out of jail."

"Very dramatic."

"Sh..." Shutting her eyes, she lifted her chin, arching her hips. He was teasing her beyond what she felt she could bear. What kind of defenses did he think she had? Truly, she couldn't take much more of this. She was a woman...flesh and blood. And right now, that flesh was sensitized; that blood was dancing. "Lick me," she whispered.

"Here?" He just missed her nipple again.

"C'mon," she begged.

Scarcely able to stand it, she reached with her hand, cupping his nape, then thrust her fingers upward until they fisted in his hair, urging him where she wanted him. He evaded her again, leaving her feeling edgier. He was so mean. So annoying. "C'mon," she murmured, sliding a hand down, pushing it into the waistband of her panties and pushing them downward on her thighs. Before she could get them to her knees, much less down her calves, his hand stilled her movements. For a moment, as his tongue wickedly stirred hot circles around her breast, licking up every bit of the chocolate, his hand glided over the back of hers. Their fingers laced. Then he brought their joined hands to the open fly of his jeans.

The heat of his erection seeped through denim and the exposed V of his briefs, feeling like fire. Pressing her hand, he urged her fingers to close around him and to explore the ridge of muscle. She squeezed until he, too, was uttering a string of deep-throated sighs. Frustrated need coursed between them.

Her other hand found his waistband, and she began to push his jeans and briefs down thighs that had gone taut, as if he was bracing himself for sensations that were sure to come. It was awkward, trying to undress while his tongue was still doing such crazy things to her. He was trailing hot, dark kisses between her breasts, blowing on the patches of liquid warmth, then sponge-bathing the slopes, the undersides.

Everything but the...

Nipple.

When he locked his mouth hard over it, a cry was wrenched from between her lips. She couldn't believe the spurt of liquid heat that arrowed down, stopping between her slightly parted legs.

Their days of lovemaking felt like years. She'd come to know just exactly what this man could do for her. She couldn't wait for the way he'd enter her, splitting her, making her feel as if she was tearing in two with pleasure of him. She couldn't wait for the way he'd thrust inside her, knowing just when to go slow. Or fast. Or to roll his hips, angling deep inside, penetrating her like a lance until they were completely joined. He'd take her this way, then that way—until her hips were writhing, leaping to greet him.

Yes, only days had passed, but her body was already attuned to his. She knew each nuance. Each quiver of muscle. After just one night in that cabin, she'd come to know how much ecstasy he could bring. He hadn't disappointed her yet. Vaguely, she wondered how she'd lived without him as her hand found—and pressured—his silken length. "Your turn," she whispered. "How's this?"

He shuddered, his voice strangled. "Oh...yes."

Against her cheek, which was pressed to his shoulder, she could feel the sweat break out on his back as slowly and deftly, she began to fondle, her hand quickening, stroking faster as his tongue gained speed, flickering against her nipple like a flame. Pure lust ran through her while his tongue drenched breasts that positively ached. They were sore beyond belief; she needed release so desperately. This had to end, she thought...and yet, she never wanted it to end at all. She wanted this pleasure to go on and on....

"Inside," she whispered simply, wanting him to come inside ever so slowly, so she could feel every inch of him as he buried himself deep. How had she lived without this kind of passion? Could a woman really get this every day of her life? "Inside," she insisted.

But he had other ideas. Standing quickly, he shucked his clothes. He was still standing, when she understood and reached for the chocolate. Yes...she needed something warm. Runny. Tasty. Rising to her knees, vaguely aware of her panties pulling tautly against her thighs, she decided there was no time to waste. She didn't remove them, but quickly used the squirt bottle, glancing up only once to see him staring down, his eyes glazed, his lips slack, his bare tanned chest rapidly rising and falling with pants of breath.

She shivered as her hand slid beneath the hot steel of the erection that would be inside her soon, and then in a way that made him growl with need, she squirted hot streams all over him, swirling the dark syrup around the head, coating the shaft. Her mouth followed. Without him even touching her, she knew she was going to explode, just from the mixture of his taste with chocolate. She arched, moaning as her pelvic bone connected with his calf. Just as his before, her tongue swirled, teasing the sensitive underside.

She was loving it. Yes, she loved giving him this. Loved the power, the shared rush of being out of control together, of making each other crazy with need. Give me everything, she thought, closing her mouth over him, taking him entirely, drawing him in, letting him cry out and drown in the pleasure. She went down on him once, twice. All the way. Until he could no longer stand it. When he spoke, the word was strangled, barely audible. "Here."

He practically threw her back onto the pillows. Grabbing her hips, he dragged her down under him. Flames from the fire behind him danced in the glowing sheen of his skin, and as he moved above her, his muscles rippled like those of a hungry jungle cat. His eyes were dazed as he grabbed a condom, ripped the foil open with his teeth and spit it out. He winced as he quickly slid it on, then his large dark hands glided up her quivering thighs. He parted them, but he didn't push the panties she wore down.

Maybe he'd meant to take the panties off. It seemed like he simply couldn't bear spending another second undressing her. She understood perfectly. Gasping, putting his elbows by her head and running his fingers deep into her hair, he crashed his mouth down on hers, meeting it—open lips to open lips. The kiss was hot and fast, their tongues wild and thrusting, rushing over each other like two flowing rivers. Lower, he thrust inside her, spreading her, making her gasp. She parted, farther and farther, the furrow deep, and she couldn't believe the pleasure that came in its wake.

Another onslaught hit. She tried to open even more for him, desperate. But her thighs were trapped, the bands of silk panties ripped, but not quite giving, and the near closure of her legs only made her tighter...making him feel bigger, so big she twisted against him, her heart racing as she took the luscious torment.

Now, she thought, her head turning on the pillow, her face blistering hot as if they'd both just dived into the fire that was two feet away. And oh...was she climbing! So was he. Higher and higher. With him so taut inside her. They were almost there. Grabbing the brass ring. Her eyes shutting in anticipation. Her body so tight around his, ready to convulse.

"This is so good," she whispered.

The climax hit them both at once, and she wished he wasn't wearing a condom. She wanted to feel his gushing heat, the full force of the explosion within her, but she was glad she could feel him pulse, his release rocking her, pouring into her, his arms enveloping her, even as she palpitated around him, the shivers of ecstasy draining her as nothing ever had before.

"Amazing," he finally whispered on a shaky breath.

And they lay there, just exactly like that for a long time, not talking, not reaching for the mugs of mulled cider that were growing cold or for the nearby afghan to cover them as their skin cooled. And then, still wrapped in each other's arms, never having said a word, they slept.

8

"WHY DO YOU KEEP manhandling me?" Signe asked the next evening, speaking softly, her voice delighted.

"I'm not," James defended.

"So you say." They'd been walking toward a French bistro she'd heard about in Times Square that was rumored not to be too touristy when they'd gotten sidetracked by a concert in Bryant Park adjacent to the New York Public Library. Smiling, she sidled in front of James and leaned backward, resting her head against his chest and reveling in the warmth as his strong forearms circled her waist. As he glided his palms over the backs of her hands, letting his fingers drop one by one between hers, she took in the symphony on stage. "Wonder what they're playing?"

"Mozart. Symphony number 4."

She laughed. "Are you sure it's not a Beethoven concerto?"

"Positive."

Her laughter tempered to a chuckle as he pressed a kiss to the top of her head. "As if you know about classical music," she chided. "Careful," she added in a barely audible tone, referring to his kiss now, "you might hurt yourself." She'd threaded her short hair with crystal beads, so that they'd sparkle, catching the early evening light.

"You look sumptuous," he whispered, leaning close to her ear.

"Big word for a park ranger."

"Your dress does wonders for my vocabulary."

"Thanks. And you look supercalifragilisticexpialidocious."

"Big word for a witch."

"How so?"

"Aren't you more used to hocus-pocus? Or abracadabra?"

"Shazam, too," she agreed. "But I'll keep those to myself. I'd hate to turn my prince back into a frog tonight, accidentally."

He laughed. "We can't have that."

She'd put on a slinky black dress. She'd bought it three years ago, when things had heated up between C.C. and her then long-term boyfriend, a hockey player. They'd gone so far as to throw a party at the Rainbow Room, during which the man had promised to propose to C.C. When he'd gotten cold feet, she'd retaliated by ending their relationship.

Signe hadn't had a chance to wear the dress since. Dots of tiny gold beads were woven into the fabric, and it had a high neckline, although the dress was open in the back. The gold shawl that slipped downward, looping over her crooked arms, was of the same harlequin pattern but with reverse coloring; the silk was studded with tiny black beads in diamond shapes. Luminous sheer gold stockings met shimmering mules, which were comfortable enough that she could stroll through the city.

"You really are sumptuous," he whispered. "I mean it."

She smiled. "And I thought you were lying."

"Cross my heart."

"So, you're an honest man."

"That surprises you?"

"You'd be one of the first."

"Now, now," he chided. "Surely your experiences with the opposite sex couldn't have been that bad."

"Not this week." She eyed him archly, adding, "So far." She squinted curiously. "And anyway, you're the one who said he'd gotten burned."

He shrugged. "No woman in particular," he assured her. "I just don't usually trust their motives."

"But you trust mine?"

He grinned. "Yeah. I do." After a moment, he added, "Despite your suspicions, I'm still holding to my position that you're really stunning."

She smiled at him. "Is *stunning* better than *sumptuous?*"

When he merely laughed, she craned her neck and glanced behind her. "You look pretty slick, too." He'd worn the gray suit from Barney's. Together with a shirt and tie, as well as the shoes they'd purchased, he could have been on the cover of a magazine. Funny, she thought now: all gussied up, he actually reminded her a little of Gorgeous Garrity. He had a similar build and coloring, and although he had brown eyes, rather than blue, his hair was similar as well, arrayed in a profusion of blonds, highlighted by time in the summer sun.

"C'mon," he suddenly said.

She frowned. "We just stopped walking. I really love listening to the symphony."

"Yeah, but..."

Grabbing her hand, he urged her away from the spot, then steered her behind a row of standing listeners and headed toward the other side of the stage. No, she decided. It really wasn't her imagination; for the past half hour, ever since they'd reached the park, he'd taken it upon himself to maneuver her toward some destination that seemed to exist only in his mind. He was doing so for no reason that she could see. She winced. It would be such a shame to suddenly realize that James had a flaw she simply couldn't live with, such as a control problem. She hated men who always had to dictate, and so far, he'd been open to her being her own person. In fact, as unlikely as it had seemed, he was turning out to be the perfect man.

And maybe she no longer cared about their superficial differences. Surely, when the week was over, he'd want to continue seeing her. She'd been quick to judge him, and while she refused to project into the future, they got along better than anyone she'd ever dated. And men could always change. Right now, he didn't even look like the same person she'd met in the Catskills.

"I was watching the concert," she reminded him, squinting at him, still looking for signs that he was transforming into "The Controlling Male." Glancing behind them, she suddenly said, "What?" Then the truth hit her. James wasn't showing signs of morphing into a control freak, after all.

"It's Perez," she guessed. That must be it. Her heart missed a beat as she thought of how sweet it was for James to protect her like this, probably because they were all dressed up and about to share a wonderful dinner together in a cozy, candlelit restaurant. He didn't want to ruin their good time. This was almost as sweet as when he'd left her at the Guggenheim, just to get her coffee. Tightening the fingers laced through his, she squeezed hard and looked up at James, feeling a rush of endearment. "He's following us again, isn't he?"

James frowned. "Uh...who?"

Confused, she said, "Detective Perez."

James still looked distracted. "Uh...no."

She squinted. "Then what's the problem?"

"Problem?"

"Is there someone behind us?" Another thought hit her, one worse than the possible exposure of a controlling personality. "An old girlfriend?" That James might need to avoid women from his past would be terrible. Or maybe he'd glimpsed someone from a previous job.

"Uh...no."

Her gaze narrowed. "Did you used to work in the city?" He seemed to know it well, but as far as she knew, he'd lived in the Catskills after growing up in Long Island.

"Uh. I have in the past. But..." He shrugged, sending her a sideways glance, and when he flashed a grin, it seemed a little contrived for her taste. "I'm just hungry and trying to move us toward the restaurant."

She didn't buy it. But she didn't counter his statement, either. The truth was, he was just too gorgeous to argue with. Pushing aside the feelings, telling herself it was nothing, she wound up merely smiling at him.

He smiled back.

Only when they reached the Forty-first Street side of the park and he headed east, toward Tudor City instead of Times Square, did she still her steps. "I thought we were going to the bistro."

"I figured we'd window-shop along Fifth Avenue," he returned easily, his fingers flexing in hers, his grip tightening.

"There's not much up there," she returned, frowning, but allowing him to lead her along the sidewalk, toward the café that was attached to the back of the library. "Only Pier One and a Swatch shop. Jewelry stores."

"I haven't looked at the lions for a while."

He was referring to the two stone lions situated on either side of the library's front staircase. She chuckled. "Again," she murmured. "Cats. It seems to be a theme of yours."

Untwining their fingers, he slipped his arm around her back, drawing her closer. For a moment, they walked in silence, and she found herself enjoying his proximity. Despite his comparative height, their strides were in synch, their gaits a comfortable match. She glanced around. At the café, no one was outside tonight—it was getting too cold—but the garden arbor was hung with brightly colored Japanese lanterns, beacons to potential customers. In just two weeks, autumn had arrived, she realized, bringing a warning sting to the air, a new crispness that promised a biting winter.

She realized he was staring at her. "Huh?"

He grinned, his grip around her back loosening as they moved away from the park. "In that black dress, you definitely look feline. Just like a kitty-cat."

Laughing, she intentionally slitted her eyes. "Meow."

"Just don't cross right in front of me."

"Don't worry. I won't hurt you. You can keep me around the house, and every time you need to cast a spell, I'll be your loyal messenger."

"Doesn't sound like you'd have much of a life of your own."

"Oh—" Lifting one of the nails she'd painted iridescent gold, she traced it down the front of his tie. "You'd be surprised. I'll always have a life of my own. We felines have our ways."

"After this week..." he began.

Her breath caught. "Yes?"

"I know the deal, Signe," he began. "We were just going to have a fling, but..."

"You don't want it to be over?"

He shook his head. "This is too good."

She could barely believe this was happening. Had love walked into her life in such an unusual way? Had she really cast a spell for Gorgeous Garrity and, instead, wound up in the bed of a park ranger whose sensual moves sent her into the stratosphere? "I was just worried..."

"That being involved with me would mean giving

up the lifestyle you want? And your own career goals." Ducking his head so he could brush his lips across hers, he said, "You're a practical woman, Signe Sargent."

She nodded. "I am," she admitted.

"I'd never take anything away from you."

It was too early to say more, but her mind was running wild with possibilities. If the man could look this good in a suit, who knew what she could do with him? And really, the more she thought about it, she realized there were ample opportunities for outdoors work in Manhattan. There were zoos, major parks, botanical gardens. He'd even mentioned the possibility of working for conservationist concerns.

His eyes had never left hers, and now he dipped his head for another kiss, his mouth warm and sweet on hers, scented by mints and good Italian coffee. Possibly, the street was no place for such shenanigans, but he felt so good, and his body was so hot and inviting in the luscious night air that, without breaking the kiss, Signe turned fully toward him. She wreathed her arms around his back, snaking them beneath the open sides of his suit jacket until her hands could clasp near his spine. Using them to draw him even nearer, she shivered as his mouth opened farther and his tongue plunged between her lips. Lazy and deep, the kiss sent spirals of need curling through her blood.

Shutting her eyes, she let her mind drift as sensation took over, edging out the sounds of the busy street, the conversations of strangers and motors of taxis. How could any one man feel so wondrously good? she thought as her back arched and her head tilted back.

Everything inside her turned as warm and runny as the thick molasses they'd had on the pancakes they'd shared in bed this morning. That was the other thing about him, she thought as his tongue swirled inside her mouth and as he nipped her lower lip playfully, his hand reaching to cup her neck. The man could cook. She'd still been asleep when he'd brought in the stack of hotcakes, drizzled with syrup and coated with butter and chopped strawberries.

Another shudder shook her bare shoulders as he slowly stroked her skin, then settled his thumb beneath her chin. Using it for leverage, he tilted her head farther up, to better drink in her lips. Heat dropped through her body by degrees, and when he angled nearer, instinctively sliding his foot between both of hers, silently asking her to part for him, she arched. She didn't exactly end the kiss then, but leaned back a fraction, so their lips just touched, and sucked an audible breath through her clenched teeth. "Maybe we should just skip dinner."

His eyes were inches away. Dreamy golden slits, they looked less brown in the twilight, and more like flamed whiskey, or the ancient amber stones she'd so often admired at the Met. "We could," he teased. "But then, how would I learn to become a more cultured individual?"

"The more I know you, the less I think you need training."

During their long hours in bed, he'd told her plenty of stories about his upbringing, and she'd shared her own. With each new unfolding saga from his life, she'd decided she liked him even more. He'd been a hellion as a kid. A black sheep. Determined to foil every expectation of a family he'd described as too upper crust and confining to contain him.

And he really did have ambition, even if it wasn't to become a white-collar professional. As it turned out, he was serious about the writing. While Signe hadn't yet read anything he'd written, nor did she really think she'd qualify as a judge, since she read mostly women's fiction, he seemed to know what he was doing and to have contacts with publishers. From watching him browse a bookstore yesterday, it was clear he followed mysteries avidly. He had a long list of favorite writers, among them people she'd also read, such as James Lee Burke and Tom Clancy, and from what they did have in common, she decided they shared a similar taste in books.

"Even if I don't need training," he murmured, his lips brushing hers again, "I still need to eat."

She nibbled his lower lip, saying, "A pity. I may just have to cast another spell on you. My magic seems to be wearing off."

"To the contrary. I'm more bewitched than ever."

"And yet you want to do something so boring as eat."

"Just for an hour or two," he promised. "And then we can go right back to bed."

"You've talked me into it," she said.

And then someone nearby called, "James! I thought that was you! We kept seeing you in the park. Every time we'd catch a glimpse of you, you'd disappear again. Your mother said it couldn't be you, however. She said nobody on earth could have forced you to get a haircut, shave that stubble and actually wear a suit."

Surprised, Signe loosened her hold on James and stepped back half a pace just as a tall, thin, silver-haired man with twinkling brown eyes tapped an ornate walking stick to the pavement a last time, removed his other hand from the deep pocket of very expensive trousers and clapped it on James's shoulder.

"If you haven't eaten, we insist you join us," said the man. "We've got a reservation at Gilda's, but she can always squeeze in two more. Your brother and Christine are meeting us, but Louise and her kids couldn't make it. That louse of a husband she married decided to fly her off to Cuba for a few days, but they'll be back in town next weekend. We're doing a last hurrah at their place in the Hamptons before they shut it down for the winter. Your aunt Anna and uncle Harold, however, are joining us, both for dinner and next weekend, and they'll love to see you."

If James needed a minute to consider his response after taking in the rambling speech, the man didn't seem to care. Presumably deciding that talking to his son was of absolutely no use, the man turned to Signe, offered a smile that had the wattage of a camera flash and asked, "How are you?"

"Uh...fine."

Just as she automatically took the hand he lifted from James's shoulder and extended to her, he said, "Garrison Jackson Garrity is my name." Chuckling at her obviously stunned expression, he jovially added, "Ask me again and I'll tell you the same. Yes, indeed, that's me. *The* Garrison Jackson Garrity. And before you murder my son," he added, now looking positively tickled pink with himself, "I want you to know that you're clearly a lovely young woman. Probably much nicer than he deserves. Definitely too nice to wind up doing jail time on his behalf. And so I just want you to know that you're not the first woman who really thought he was a park ranger."

That said, the man slid his hand beneath Signe's elbow and gently, deftly, turned her, guiding her in the direction of the park again saying, "Don't worry, Miss...uh..."

"Sargent," she supplied, feeling dumbfounded.

"You're in good hands. Myself and my wife, Jacqueline, intend to buy you a most exquisite dinner, if only for being so kind as to put up with the supposed park ranger we've spawned."

9

EXQUISITE HARDLY COVERED the dinner, Signe thought an hour later, watching as three sprigs of lettuce arrived. This was, seemingly, what Gilda Goddard, the eatery's owner, meant when she'd offered Signe a salad. After appetizers so small that they could have fit onto the head of a thimble had come a bowl of soup, in which something floated that looked suspiciously like eyes. Even if the mystery morsels hadn't tasted marvelous, which they had, it still didn't change the fact that Gorgeous Garrity was seated just across the linen-covered table from Signe.

As it turned out, he didn't even remember her. At first, Signe had thought it was a joke, but even now, an hour later, no glimmer of recognition had yet stirred in his eyes. He hadn't even reacted when she'd given her name. Apparently a flirtation with a waitress didn't carry much weight in Gorgeous Garrity's memory bank. She should have guessed! And his brother was even worse!

Fuming, slapping away James's hand every time he tried to settle it on her leg, she tried not to recall their conversation outside the Guggenheim when, at any point, he could have quickly interjected something about his true parentage. Only moments ago, she'd been considering a future with him.

She simply couldn't believe that "Aunt Anna" had turned out to be Anna Garrity. Or that the brother he'd played with, and been staying with in Manhattan, was Gorgeous. Or that the his Long Island childhood home hadn't been in one of the middle-class enclaves, but rather directly on the water where old money lived in what amounted to palaces. What a liar! James Garrity had been born with a silver spoon between the lips that had been kissing her senseless all week, and he'd never dropped so much as a hint. Not even when they'd been doing that over-the-top sexy thing with all that gooey chocolate!

Signe blew out a surreptitious breath, not even sure why she hadn't yet risen, tossed her napkin onto her antique china plate, turned and strode imperiously from the restaurant. What a paradox. She'd thought she wanted a Garrity, and now she had one, but only when the relationship was based in his lies. Given the circumstances, she wasn't the least bit thrilled about her chance to get this insider's view into the dining habits of the rich and famous.

As near as she could tell, Gilda's was one of those hidden, exorbitantly priced eateries that were peopled by a strange mix of Hollywood celebrities and monied American aristocracy dating back to the *Mayflower*. This was one of those places where the Queen of England could dine in peace without having a ring of dark-suited bodyguards hovering around, to dispel the crowd of gawkers. There was no hostess, no bills, no menus.

Absolutely no paparazzi was allowed to lurk outside. Gilda herself decided what everyone would eat.

And should ever the restaurant be listed in a guide such as Zagat, alerting average-Joe-citizens such as Signe to its existence, Signe got the distinct impression that Zagat would disappear overnight. Just like some mobsters and Jimmy Hoffa: the guide would simply vanish without a trace.

She felt James leaning close. Breath that had felt as shivery as moon dust just an hour before was now annoying her beyond belief. She'd consider flinging her cosmopolitan into his face, just because she was sure no one had ever created a scene in Gilda's, but such a move was simply beneath her.

"I know you're mad at me," he whispered.

"You're what?" She glared at him. "A rocket scientist? Or was that a brain surgeon?" Even as she whispered the words in a hushed tone so that only he could hear, she silently cursed him for forcing her to stoop to such ridiculously childish defenses. She felt like an idiot. How could she have let him play her this way? How many park rangers carried Mont Blanc pens and knotted a tie perfectly without using a mirror?

Once more, she pushed away the offending hand that kept trying to creep up her leg. What a user! Yes, he was just like his brother. She stared across the table, taking in the newly wedded couple, who were rambling on about playing tennis at the sister's house—apparently Gorgeous and James had a sister named Louise Amherst who had a summer place in the Hamptons, not to mention a jet-setting husband and two rambunctious boys in grade and middle school.

"You wouldn't believe who's bought near Louise," murmured Christine, her dark, perfectly plucked eyebrows furrowing.

And you wouldn't believe who's about to leave this table, Signe thought, feeling as if her head might explode while Christine began to demean the television celebrities who were moving into Louise's ritzy neighborhood and supposedly ruining it.

"At least we don't have any rock stars yet," Gorgeous remarked, as if to indicate they could expect that to happen any day soon. Clearly, from his tone, he felt that the world—or at least the Hamptons— was going to hell in a handbasket.

As Signe listened, she sighed, just glad she'd been able to deflect the conversation from herself. Perhaps her smartest move had been to lie, saying she didn't work. Oh, she hated lying, especially since she wasn't very good at it. It made her almost as bad as the Garritys. But what other option did she have?

It was sorely tempting, of course, to tell the Garritys that she was their son's paid escort, and that he'd signed up for a makeover, hoping to give himself some culture. A makeover, she'd happily inform the elder Garritys, that both their sons obviously needed, since both were incapable of anything even vaguely resembling human honesty.

At least, since everyone thought she was unemployed, they were assuming she lived on a trust fund, which was good. Or, at least Signe thought so until Anna Garrity began a long monologue, trying to discern from which Sargents Signe hailed, the Boston or the Dallas Sargents, the answer to which was neither.

Not only did Signe not hail from those Sargents, she'd never even heard of them.

Yes, usually she'd be taking mental notes on every nuance, absorbing everything from the conversation, to the make of the silverware, to the clothes people wore, so that she could share all the juicy details with her girlfriends, who'd want to live vicariously through this, but not tonight.

Instead she stared at Christine, feeling an uncharacteristic rush of menace. True, Gorgeous's wife was just as breathtaking as he. Luminous eyes were set in a perfectly oval face. Large lips were faintly glossed in a bronze that suited her olive skin. And while Signe couldn't see the whole of her dress, it was frilly, light and airy, of layered chiffon. Just looking at her would make any admirer use words such as *divine*.

And yet, Christine was so shallow! Having barely touched her food, she hung on to her husband's arm, leaving the impression that she could listen to him talk about his tennis game until kingdom come. Her monologues were scarcely more than strung-together clichés! How could this be possible?

Fortunately, Garrison Garrity, whom Signe was deciding she liked immensely, didn't seem impressed. Beneath his eyelids, he seemed to be surveying Signe, just as she was him, trying to discern her relationship to his son.

Jacqueline, on the other hand, seemed to concentrate on her daughter-in-law, and Signe couldn't help but feel relieved that she didn't seem overly impressed by Christine, either. After all, Signe would like to walk away from this dinner feeling that at least one member of the Garrity family had some common sense. She'd followed their comings and goings in the society column, and it would be nice if she could part with at least one illusion intact.

Though, it was hard to read Jacqueline. And James had sure fooled her. But Jacqueline, like James's aunt, Anna Garrity, did look surprisingly practical. Both women wore their shoulder-length blond hair straight and sported very little makeup, and their suits would have been appropriate to wear to an upscale office.

With his dark hair, tall build and square jaw, Harold Garrity, the uncle who'd thankfully not yet connected Signe to his missing Eros statue, looked a lot like an aging Cary Grant; however, he was unfortunately not nearly as charming. Mostly, he spent his time gazing down at his own tie. He'd lift it, examine it, then let it fall. Occasionally, as if that particular diversion was starting to fail him, he'd pick at his pearl tie pin instead, as if he half suspected the pearl's luminous silvery exterior would turn out to be nothing more than a delicately applied coat of paint.

He perked up when Jacqueline shifted her attention to James. Curiously eyeing him, as if he'd long been a mystery to her, Jacqueline said, "What have you been up to?" Given her faintly puzzled tone, she could have been consulting an oracle.

"Not much." He shrugged, once more trying to settle a hand on Signe's thigh. "Signe and I have been all over New York this week. We took in some theater. The Klein exhibit at the Guggenheim."

At that, everyone looked interested. Uncle Harold said, "The Klein exhibit?"

James nodded, snaking his hand along the back of Signe's chair, a move that only served to further annoy her, since he well knew she wouldn't publicly slap it away. She sent him an acid glance as he said, "She'd heard his lecture at Columbia, and since she has an excellent art history background, we—"

Jacqueline gasped, her eyes shifting to Signe. "You attended Mr. Klein's lecture?"

Realizing she was no longer going to be able to play the wallflower, Signe nodded, trying to keep the thread of anger from her voice. "Yes. I did."

"We couldn't attend," Jacqueline apologized as the main course was served. "We were in Australia."

"Oh, please, Jacqueline! Klein's nothing more than a two-bit illustrator," Uncle Harold declared, sounding thoroughly disgusted. "People such as him are destroying art in America, and you know it!"

Ever since Christina's speech about the newly monied celebrities moving into Louise's neighborhood, Signe had about had it with the whole family. "Hardly," she defended, probably more hotly than she should have. "Klein's very misunderstood, in my view. While it's true he attended the Pittsburgh Art Institute and has blue-collar roots, I should also point out that he's brought that experience to his work in a way that few others have. What seems mere illustration to you, may be something you simply don't fully understand, Mr. Garrity." Ah. There, she'd done it now: implied that a Garrity was so dense as to not understand illustration work.

Taking a deep breath, and vaguely registering that she was plunging into ever hotter water, Signe continued her defense of the artist—only to have the table turn silent, then come to life again—with all the Garritys arguing and taking various positions.

"Bravo!" approved Jacqueline when the talk died down. Somehow, the genuinely warm smile she sent toward Signe gave no comfort. In fact, it made Signe wish she hadn't opened her mouth in the first place. Escaping James would be much easier if his mother hated her, she decided, and after tonight, she was definitely not going to see the man again.

"You're quite something!" Jacqueline complimented. "I should have known. Any woman who can make my son stroll through Midtown and listen to the symphony while wearing a suit...and the haircut is marvelous."

When Signe hazarded another glance at James, she had to admit she understood his mother's position. James looked even better than his brother, Gorgeous. Had he decided not to slum it as a park ranger, the man could have ruled Manhattan. Maybe even the world. He'd been born to the manor. And for whatever inexplicable reason, he'd walked away.

Why? Signe wondered. Gritting her teeth, she pushed aside the question. James Garrity's motivations were none of her business! She didn't want to know! She wanted to get up from the table, tell him she didn't appreciate being lied to, even if he was a Garrity, and then she wanted to stride out of this restaurant! Only by doing so could she restore her own sense of equilibrium, not to mention her self-respect.

Pressing her hand to her heart, James's mother excitedly continued, "You're a genius when it comes to art, Signe. I'm so impressed. And you know so much about history! You must just love the subject! Where on earth did James find you?"

Signe braced herself for the inevitable queries about where she'd gone to school, knowing the expected answer would be something Ivy League, probably Yale or Harvard, but the question never came. Just as she was exhaling a sigh of relief, still hoping to get out of this dinner without some further embarrassing incident, Uncle Harold loudly cleared his throat and said, "Let's just hope Klein has the common sense not to lend his pieces to the Metropolitan Museum!"

The table exploded, with everyone talking at once. Finally, Jacqueline's voice rose over the others. "Now, don't be ridiculous, Harold. Your statue was insured. And Detective Perez is exploring every possible avenue. He's a veteran. He's been on the force for twenty years, and is reputed to be quite competent."

"Reputed," echoed Harold significantly, nodding his head up and down vehemently.

"Exactly," added Gorgeous. "He can't be trusted. And Edmond Styles needs to be replaced. As you know, I like to spend a few minutes every day viewing the collections." He flashed his mother and father an ingratiating smile. "Especially those offered by our family."

Nothing more than Gorgeous's obsequious tone was enough to set Signe's teeth on edge. It was as if

Gilda had placed a chalkboard at the front of the restaurant, and was now busy scraping her long, unob-
trusively painted nails downward on it. Signe
thought she'd gag! The more the family talked, the
clearer it became. Everyone at the table had their eye
on the elder Garrison Garrity's money.

And Gorgeous was the worst! It was no wonder
Garrison seemed to secretly favor James, even though
Gorgeous and Christine didn't seem to be the least bit
aware of the fact. The trouble was, though, that James
had opted out of the family business. Signe almost
felt sorry for his father, who was left having to make
do with Gorgeous, who was now running his empire.
Oh, before this, she'd thought Gorgeous was brilliant,
but now that she'd seen the family in action, it was
clear that Garrison wished he was relying on his
other, more recalcitrant son. At least James had a
mind of his own.

Why had he walked away from it all? Signe
doubted it was so that he could pursue his writing
ambitions. After all, he could write in his spare time,
no matter what else he did. So...why? It didn't make
sense. Nor was it her business, she reminded herself.
As soon as she downed the last spoonful of what she
was sure would prove to be a delectable dessert—if
Signe even made it that long—she was going to rise
and leave. She was never going to look back, either.

"Yes," Gorgeous was saying, "Styles needs to go.
Let's not forget that he gave the responsibility for ac-
tivating those alarms to a waitress. Who would believe it? He made absolutely no effort to protect Uncle
Harold's statue."

"And it was Eros, too," Christine said.

"Who knows what perverted person might have stolen such an object, hoping to improve his sex life," said Gorgeous.

"Or hers," Signe couldn't help but say. "Let's not be sexist here." Besides, she wanted to add, but didn't, if they presumed a pervert had stolen the statue, how did that reflect on the Garritys? After all, they were the people who *owned* the supposedly perverse artifact!

Really, this had gone too far! If Gorgeous persisted, Edmond really could get fired, since Gorgeous was on the board of directors. It was bad enough that Signe had made such an error—if she really had, which she doubted—but it was hardly Edmond's fault. He'd been trying to give her an opportunity, one she'd very much deserved.

"Please," she suddenly said. "Edmond Styles is a remarkable administrator." Signe had always wanted to work for him. Even now, after he'd temporarily laid her off, she didn't resent him in the least.

Jacqueline looked at her with renewed interest, as if to say the social circle had just closed a notch. "You know Edmond?"

Cringing, Signe considered. Edmond's relationship with the Garritys was something of a mystery to her, but because of their involvement with the museum, she knew he met with some of them frequently. Beyond that, she'd never much wondered about it—as a café waitress, she'd figured she was too subordinate to worry over such matters—but now she supposed Edmond and the Garritys might know each other better than she'd assumed. Finally, she said, "I know him well enough to speak to."

Jacqueline continued squinting, now trying to place Signe, as if she'd probably met everyone who knew Edmond. "Know him from..."

"Signe worked at the Met for a spell," James explained, nothing more than the sound of his voice sending a thread of nearly murderous anger coursing through her blood. If the rest of his family didn't require so much of her mental energy, Signe would have the available head space to better decide how to handle James when this grueling ordeal was over. Her heart turned over unexpectedly, feeling as if it really had wrenched inside her chest cavity. Had she really stood outside, just moments ago in James's arms, talking about possibly making future plans for him? How could it end this way?

Jacqueline was staring at her expectantly. She shook her head, frowning. "I thought I knew all the curators."

Deciding not to explain that she'd been slugging coffee, and most of it to Jacqueline's own flirtatious son, who, as it turned out, hadn't even remembered her name, Signe skirted the question and simply said, "Dismissing Edmond would be a grave error. Few people care for art as much as he does. He's been at the Met for years and has done a wonderful job."

"You're quite the champion," remarked Garrison Garrity, as if in an aside. "First Klein, now Styles."

She'd also whipped James into shape, something that had clearly stunned everyone. It took everything she had, but she refused to look at him. Maybe she couldn't. If she did, she wasn't quite sure she'd trust herself not to cry. Moments ago, outside, care and kindness had flowed between them, but she hadn't even known who he really was....

"Be that as it may," Gorgeous was saying, "but Uncle Harold's right, and at the next board meeting, I can only say I intend to argue for his removal."

"Security is always your pet peeve," said Jacqueline. "Don't penalize Edmond because of it."

"Good boy," said Harold approvingly, ignoring Jacqueline. "You're a chip off the old block."

Truly, these people were beyond the pale, playing with people's lives this way. From what Signe knew of Edmond Styles's background, it was much like her own. He'd worked hard to pursue his dream of a city life, and a job working with beautiful fine art. "Edmond Styles, I'm sure, has taken care of the internal problems."

"On what information do you have this?" asked Harold.

Signe thought hard. "On my own." Unable to take this any longer, she rose from her seat and placed her napkin beside her untouched million-dollar entrée, just the way she'd been fantasizing about doing all night. "I'm the employee that Harold Styles asked to flip that alarm switch. I'm also sure I did so. However, someone did steal the statue of Eros, and in an effort to ensure the containment of the problem, he dismissed me." Her gaze bored directly into Harold's. "Are you satisfied now?"

There was a long, stunned silence.

"Please sit down, dear," said Jacqueline, her eyes

wide, as if she'd never witnessed such an unusual scene.

"I'm so sorry," Signe managed to say. "But your son and I really did have other dinner plans tonight."

Jacqueline looked faintly wounded. "I'm so sorry if we impinged in any way. My husband and I only wanted you to join us—"

Signe shook her head. "Not at all. It's just that I needed to be home a half an hour ago," she lied. "And—" Before James could rise, she clamped a hand on his shoulder to ensure he wouldn't follow her. "I think it would be best if James stays and takes this opportunity to visit with you, since he hasn't done so in a while." She smiled down at him sweetly, fluttering her eyelashes. "He was just saying earlier how much he's missed you."

"Wait." Jacqueline reached a hand to stop her. "There must be some mistake. As I said, I thought I knew all the curators at the Met, but obviously I don't. I can tell, however, just from talking to you, that you're immensely qualified, and you also think very highly of Edmond, whom I dearly love. I don't know why we've never met, but I'm sure he only let you go because he was trying to please my son, who's always overly interested in the museum's security."

"Overly," said Gorgeous. "Look at what's happened."

"There's just been some misunderstanding," Jacqueline repeated. "Gorgeous was under the impression that Edmond had actually allowed a waitress to handle the art—"

Signe's heart was pounding double time. "He did."

Jacqueline's hand rose to her throat. "Excuse me?"

"I am—or was—a waitress in the café"

Gorgeous uttered a soft gasp. "Oh, God. I knew she looked familiar."

It was about time Gorgeous figured it out. Signe didn't bother to glare at him. It just wasn't worth the effort.

"A waitress?" Jacqueline stared into space a moment, her entire body so still that she could have been a mannequin. She looked as if she was listening hard to an internal voice that would tell her what to do next. It was as if she believed that the ghosts of cultured women had been imbedded in her subconsciousness, and if she just remained utterly motionless, Jackie Onassis or Eleanor Roosevelt would offer her something gracious to say.

Signe had a half a mind to offer her a Ouija board.

Instead, she gave into the urge to glare at Gorgeous; he'd piped down, seemingly remembering the flirtation, and the fact that his wife was on his arm tonight. "Because Edmond was considering promoting me into the archives department," Signe continued, "he gave me some responsibility guarding the displays the night the statue was stolen. Again, I can only assure you that I'm positive I flipped that alarm switch."

Jacqueline had recovered her senses. "I believe you," she announced. Quickly, she reached into her pocket, drew out an embossed card and tiny gold pen, with which she started scribbling. Once done, she handed the card to Signe. "Here. It's my daughter Louise's address out in the Hamptons. We're all going out this weekend. Edmond has a cottage about an hour away, and he's to come for afternoon tea this Friday. I asked him, expressly, because I wanted to discuss the family's contribution to some upcoming exhibits, and because he feels so badly about the disappearance of the statue. Please," she insisted. "You must come out. It'll be too late to return to the city, so pack a bag."

What was happening? Signe wanted nothing more than to turn on her heel and leave. The longer she'd stayed, the stranger the whole encounter got. "Thank you so much for the kind offer," she forced herself to say, since the thought of bunking down under the same roof as James would be impossible after this. Unless, of course, James vowed not to go to the Hamptons. But then, that would require talking to him privately, which Signe was determined not to do. Besides, he'd already proved himself a liar. Who could trust him now?

James. What was she going to do about him? He was so dreamy. So sexy. So good in bed.

Pushing aside all thoughts of him, she sighed. This really was her own fault. In a full week, she'd never even asked his last name. And that was so strange! She frowned. It simply didn't make sense. She was the cool-headed one of her girlfriends; the practical, logical one who didn't want wild sex so much as to settle down! At least that was usually true. They were right about her being a quasi prude, at least by New York standards. She'd never slept with a man unless she'd known something about his family history. In fact, she'd often known social security numbers and bank balances before the big event.

So, what had happened? She'd never even thought to ask James about those things. And how had she overlooked not knowing a man's last name? Maybe it was because this was supposed to be her one carefree fling, and yet...

"Tea sounds wonderful," Signe managed to say again. "However, I wouldn't feel right about imposing...."

"If you want a job, you'd better," warned Garrison Garrity, suddenly chuckling as if no dinner he'd ever attended had delighted him more.

True. Signe blew out a breath. The man knew she was caught between a rock and a hard place. "Perhaps if I arrive during the tea," she ventured, her eyes studiously avoiding James's.

"You need to come for the weekend." Jacqueline was adamant. "There's so much room. And since I do so much work with the Met, I'd really like to know you more. As intelligently as you spoke about Klein's work, it's clear you have a very bright future. Besides, I'm not sure how long the conversation with Edmond will take. In fact, I'll also call Detective Perez."

"Oh, please. No. I'm sure this can be handled without my help." Things were really snowballing.

Jacqueline didn't even seem to notice. "We'll all be able to get an update. Since you're concerned in the matter, you'll need to hear all the progress...."

The woman was twisting everything around! If these weren't Garritys, Signe might actually think the mother was matchmaking. Who knew? Maybe she was. After all, Signe really had managed to turn her son out in a suit and tie.

"There's so much room at Louise's," she repeated.

"My, my," said Garrison, addressing Signe. "I think my wife would be happy to give you a whole wing of my daughter's house. You'll have it all to yourself, my dear."

"I just want to make sure Edmond understands you're a friend of ours," persisted Jacqueline. She paused delicately. "A friend of *James's*."

Great. She *was* matchmaking. Worse, Signe didn't exactly want her ex-boss railroaded into rehiring her. As paradoxical as it was, she wound up saying, "I stand by the decision Edmond has made." Not that she'd exactly enjoyed getting canned.

"Of course you do," Jacqueline soothed. "That's why it's so important that we straighten out this whole silly mess. I'll have Detective Perez drive out, just as I promised. Now, how's that? And Harold can come...."

Now Jacqueline Garrity sounded as if she was arranging place cards at one of her parties. "That sounds just lovely," Signe said. "Really, it does, Mrs. Garrity, but I'm sure that as soon as Detective Perez finds that statue, everything will fall into place for me."

"Let's face it," Jacqueline said kindly. "It may be gone forever, Signe."

She had a point, as much as Signe hated to admit it. No doubt about it, these people were from the Dale Carnegie school of "how to win friends and influence people." They were making Signe offers she couldn't refuse. She needed to face some realities. James had lied and she never intended to see him again, but with a nod from Jacqueline Garrity, Signe could even bypass a stint in the archives department and wind up as a curator before her thirtieth birthday. Not that she was using Mrs. Garrity, but she wanted the matter cleared up. She knew she'd flipped the switch on the alarm and had been falsely accused.

Regarding Edmond having his authority overridden by Jacqueline Garrity, it was just as possible that Edmond had only laid her off because he'd been getting pressure from Gorgeous. If so, that meant he'd be happy to hire her back, under these circumstances.

Until she talked to Edmond, Signe wouldn't be able to gauge his feelings, and that meant having afternoon tea with the Garritys in the Hamptons. If James happened to show—which given her blatant rejection, she doubted he would—she'd have devised a strategy between now and then to deal with him. Surely, after the way he'd lied, he wouldn't have the nerve to show his face.

"All right," Signe finally said, squeezing James's shoulder again, hard. "You need not get up," she reminded. Then to Jacqueline she added, "I'll see you then."

James rose, anyway. "Signe."

A look from Garrison stopped him. "I'll walk you to the door, Ms. Sargent, and make sure you're safely in a taxi," Garrison said. Shooting his son a glance, he merely added one word in warning. "James."

Nothing else was necessary. Signe was astonished to see that James actually seated himself. He might be the family black sheep, but clearly Garrison's power still held sway. And while Garrison might have handed his business over to Gorgeous, he still wore the pants in the family.

If Signe hadn't been so upset about James's deception, she might have laughed. The dapper Garrison cut quite a figure. He was jovial and full of fun. Still, as with most places in the world, money could so easily become the bottom line. Ultimately, he always got the last word. "Thank you, Mr. Garrity," Signe managed to say as she felt his hand slide under her elbow.

"I wouldn't want you to think we Garritys have no manners, Ms. Sargent," he returned.

Given his amusement, she was half tempted to inform him about his son's enrollment in charm school, but she refrained. She needed to process what had just happened. And now, since they were away from the table, she finally could.

They were almost at the front door when her feet stilled. When she stopped moving, she felt, rather than saw, Garrison turn toward her, his brow furrowing with concern. "You look as if you've seen a ghost," he said. "Are you all right, Ms. Sargent?"

"I'm fine," she managed, recovering enough to propel herself forward again. But she wasn't! Ever since they'd met Garrison Garrity on the street, too many things had been happening, but now it was all catching up. She'd really just left the man who'd been sharing her bed. He was really still sitting behind her, gaping at her back as she left the restaurant on the arm of his father. And he was really a Garrity.

Anger twisted inside her, but not before she felt the

hard knot forming in her throat, too. She could barely swallow around it. Everything in her mind protested: no, no, no. It had been such a perfect week. She'd come to imagine that it would never end. Hours of unbridled sex had done something strange to her brain, turning it to mush, so much so that she hadn't even asked for his last name. How could he have led her on like that? Just as with his brother, maybe she was just some little nothing. A fling with a waitress who was easy to toss away. And yet, he'd gotten to her. She didn't want to walk away...leave what they'd shared behind.

And yet how could she do otherwise? After all, she didn't even know him. As far as she was concerned, this invalidated their every moment together. If she'd known who he really was, everything would have been so different....

All that, however, was not what had stopped her in her tracks.

Rather, she'd suddenly remembered the spell she'd cast in the Catskills. Searching her mind, she tried to remember exactly what she'd said in the spell. No...she hadn't specified *which* Garrity she wanted sex with, much less to marry, she realized now, nor had she divulged to whom the handkerchief belonged. As she considered the idea that the spell had actually worked, her knees weakened. She and James had joked about it, but he'd never found out that the object of the spell had been a Garrity.

Just as her knees buckled, Garrison caught her. "Don't worry," he teased with a kind smile. "I always have this effect on women."

Both he and his son, Signe thought shakily. But if James's omission about his identity invalidated their relationship, the fact that a wiccan spell had brought them together was even worse. She'd begun to fall for him. And he with her. She knew it.

And now, no matter how intense the connection between them, it wasn't real. Thinking hard, Signe tried to remember the name of the witches shop she'd seen on West Fourth Street. She could almost visualize it—its windows shrouded in black, the display case full of leather-bound books, voodoo dolls, tarot cards and candles.

Surely they'd know how to reverse a little white magic.

10

"MRS. AMHERST AND THE children will be home from the beach at any moment. The kids begged to go this afternoon," Louise's maid, Gabriella, prattled amiably as she showed Signe to a guest room. Glancing toward a window, she continued, "It's too cold to swim, really, unless you're James, of course, who enjoys taking dips in the freezing cold, but Louise's boys, Steven and Charles, said they wanted to play football near the water. Anyway, everyone will be here soon. Both boys need to change for tea." Pausing, she sighed. "It looks as if a storm's brewing out there."

"It does, doesn't it?" asked Signe, glancing toward the darkening sky as she set down her bag. Because the well-appointed room was decorated in red and white, she felt as if she was standing inside a huge Valentine card. Thick red carpeting covered the floors, a double bed was spread with a white duvet, and while the lower section of the walls were painted white, the upper sections, which were separated by white molding graced with heart cutouts, were papered in a red-and-white floral print.

"I wasn't sure what to wear for tea...." Signe glanced down at the simple beige suit she'd chosen, hoping it was right. She had absolutely no idea what high tea with the Garritys might entail, or how she'd handle the seemingly inevitable encounter with James, and just in case she was wrong about the outfit, she'd come prepared with a few others in her suitcase.

"You look perfect," Gabriella assured her, filling Signe with relief.

"Oh, good. Thank you for saying so."

"Mr. Amherst is, unfortunately, still away on business," Gabriella continued. "And neither Mr. Styles nor Detective Perez have arrived yet, but I'll let you know when they do. Otherwise, tea will be ready in an hour, so if you'd like to take the time to unpack..."

"Thank you," Signe murmured.

As soon as Gabriella left, Signe leaned against the closed door, exhaling a nervous breath, and then she reached for the large manilla envelope she'd brought. Quickly crossing the room, she lifted the edge of a curtain, peeked around the side of it and stared downward, through a window, onto the landscaped lawn below.

He was here! Right beneath the window, James was talking to his uncle Harold, clearly not giving a rat's behind as to Signe's feelings. Again. Yes, she should have guessed the man wouldn't do the gentlemanly thing and comply with her obvious, if unstated, request that he not be present at his sister's house this weekend. He knew very well that Signe had been forced into the position of coming to tea against her will. When her eyes slid to the white duvet on the bed, which was so similar to the duvet on her own, it brought a flood of memories of James's lovemaking.

As if touched by a magic wand, she could feel strong hands gliding slowly, effortlessly, down her legs until they reached her ankles. She imagined James ever so gently caressing the arched insteps of her feet, massaging them until the warmth of his touch sizzled on her skin. He was naked, of course. And as he moved toward her, his bare skin emanating heat, she moaned. His answer was the steely length of his body as he lay on top of her, then a soft, satisfied male grunt of pleasure as he used his knee to open her legs. When he entered her, she released a shudder that shook her whole body....

Every time she imagined such things, it seemed so real.

"Great," she whispered, wishing he didn't look quite so good. He'd been swimming, probably hanging around with his sister and nephews, and despite the relative coolness of the day, he was wearing sandals and a loose-fitting white shirt open over dark trunks, the legs of which nearly hit his knees. She also wished that his voice hadn't sounded on her answering machine quite so many times this week. He kept asking if he could see her, to explain why he'd omitted the truth about his background, and while she'd sat beside the phone listening, with her hand on the receiver, she hadn't been about to pick it up.

Not even after he sent a four-foot-tall arrangement of tropical flowers. He'd arrived at her apartment the next day, too, talking through the closed door, saying, "I know you're in there, Signe. Please, I understand why you're angry, but why don't you let me come inside so we can talk about this?"

She'd stood on the other side of the door, holding her breath, so he wouldn't guess she was there, and she'd stared through the peephole until he'd finally given up and gone away. His persistence had convinced her that he hadn't been using her. No matter how their affair had begun, he wanted her back. He really liked her.

But it just wasn't meant to be. Now she glanced away from him, quickly taking in her rental car, which was parked near a fountain situated in the middle of a circular driveway. Wincing, she hoped James hadn't witnessed her arrival. Usually C.C. drove when Signe and her friends went anywhere, so it had taken her a full hour to find a driver's license that she'd supposed had expired. Discovering it hadn't, she'd rented a car, but her driving skills were rusty, and she'd known better than to ask for detailed directions about vehicle operation from the rental company; if they'd refused to rent her the car, then she'd have to have called James to ask for a ride. Or Detective Perez or Edmond Styles. All of which were unthinkable options.

Fortunately, somewhere between the city and the Hamptons, she'd gotten the hang of safely passing in lanes that looked too narrow, even for a compact, and she'd made it up the driveway of Louise Amherst's home in one piece, if puttering in a series of embarrassing fits and starts.

Now her eyes drifted over the vast, freshly mowed lawn that ended in a hill that sloped gracefully to the ocean. While she couldn't see Louise and her sons, the ocean was visible, the waves beginning to kick up and wash ashore in darkly foaming breakers. When she peered at the blanket of gray fog more closely, she was surprised to find oddly patterned patches of blue. Surreal and powdery, the color breaking through was overly bright, like Technicolor.

"Strange mojo," she whispered. *Eerie.*

Which was just as well, given what Signe was about to do. Dropping the curtain, she ripped the leaf from the envelope and began emptying the contents onto the bed: first came a bell, book and candle, then a handful of bunched straw and something the witches on West Fourth Street had called a lover's smudge stick; it was a wrapped bundle of herbs that smelled mostly of sage, which she was to burn. The object of her affection, meaning James, needed to be within one hundred yards for the spell reversal to work, according to the witches. Gauging carefully, she figured James was only thirty feet away, and whispered, "Strike while the iron's hot."

After choosing a clear area in the middle of the plush red carpet, she disentangled the straw pieces and laid them end to end, forming her magic circle. Supposedly, these were supercharged mystical straw strands taken from a broom once ridden by a witch so famous that the women in the shop wouldn't even tell Signe her name.

Standing inside the circle, Signe flipped open the book of spells to the correct page, then she headed for her suitcase and took out a dinner plate. Having already prepared it by wrapping it in tinfoil, she laid it in the circle to use as an incense burner, placed the smudge stick on the foil and lit it.

"Great," she muttered with worry as the sage caught fire. "It smells exactly like marijuana." She wasn't a smoker of the stuff, but she'd been to enough parties in college to recognize the scent. Then she whispered, "Oh. The bell."

After heading for her suitcase again, she returned once more, shut her eyes as she'd been instructed and took ten deep breaths. Opening her eyes, she lifted the bell and gave it three hard rings, surprised at the tone. They hadn't warned her it would be so loud! Or that the air would become so smoky! Already her eyes were stinging against the stream of thick gray that was rising from the smudge stick. Smoke was quickly filling the room. Should she open the window and start over? No, that would be even worse, she decided. James and his uncle Harold would see smoke pouring out of Louise's second-floor bedroom, and hell really *would* break loose....

"Just hurry," she muttered, waving her hand to clear the air. Lifting the bell, she rang it three more times, intoning, "With this bell begins my spell. Back we go. An old spell to undo."

So far, so good. Except she could barely see through the cloud of smoke in which she now stood. And worse...she suddenly hesitated. Did she really want to reverse the spell, after all? James was obviously falling for her. Despite her worry over whether or not he'd just been using her, not wanting her to know he was a Garrity in case she might become interested in him for the wrong reasons, he'd continued to call her. Shouldn't she be thrilled? So what if he'd lied? Some women forgave their husbands for worse, right? She'd heard stories from the New Jersey wiccans that would chill anyone's blood.

And all James had done was tell a little white lie. She didn't even know why! He cared for her! And yet, she had to face the truth. All that great sex only happened because she'd cast a spell to get in bed with a Garrity. Obviously, it had worked, which meant absolutely nothing about her and James's affair had been...well, *natural.*

Yes, it was very tempting not to reverse the spell, she thought, blinking rapidly, her eyes stinging from all the infernal smoke. But then, even if things progressed with her and James...even if the world's greatest lover wanted to marry her someday, she'd always know he didn't really love her. Whatever he felt was only because of magic....

Forcing her mind to her task again, she rang the bell, whispering, "Three rings I give thee. From the old spell, free me." Yes, she was going through with this, but it was so terrible! She was conscious of her eyes stinging again, now from unshed tears, not smoke.

Setting the bell down beside the candle, she lifted the spell book, and carefully read from the folded paper inside, which she'd read in the Catskills. After perusing the original spell, she brought the book nearly beneath her nose, so she could read the words that would end her and James's affair. She whispered, her throat aching from emotion:

The die was cast
The words all spoken
And the spell ne'er to be broken
It was all arranged
But now things have changed
I came by Garrity
So unfairly
So shift the magic
Forget the logic
This new spell I give thee
From all old spells, free me
Show me your sign

She tensed, waiting to feel...well, *something* that would indicate this had worked. According to the spell, she was to receive some sign. A shiver maybe. Or a ka-boom. *Something.*

And then water hit her.

It came full force, out of the blue. An inexplicable waterfall from the ceiling. Simultaneously, a loud, shrill sound emanated from above. Blinking her eyes against the spray of water, she spluttered, spitting water from her lips as she set down the book. "What the...?"

Waving away smoke, Signe sidestepped, instinctively pushing back her drenched hair from her face and heading in the direction of the window, which she could no longer see. Only when she opened it and saw smoke streaming outside did she hear a crack of thunder. The sound reverberated through her, as if lightning had struck iron. The sky outside opened, and all at once, rain was showering down. Feeling vaguely disoriented, she wondered if she'd only *thought* she was standing inside, when *really* she'd been outside all along, but that was impossible. Nevertheless, it seemed to be raining inside!

"Oh," she murmured. A smoke alarm and sprinkler system had been ingeniously obscured by the light fixture. "Of course," she whispered. The Garritys—or in this case, a Garrity who'd married an Amherst—would keep their home well protected. Whirling, she frantically tried to push the smoke through the window. "It really does smell like marijuana," she whispered in horror, although anybody who actually smoked this much of the stuff would be loopy for their rest of their life. "Shoo," she urged the smoke, "get out of here!"

It was too late. Hearing the door open, she turned to face it. A crowd was outside! The smoke had cleared enough that she could see James, his parents, Gorgeous, Christine, Harold and Louise. She fought not to plaster a bright grin on her face and perkily say, "Gee. Are we missing anyone?"

"Really," she managed to shout instead, straining to be heard over the alarm and the deluge of rain outside. "I'm so sorry. I can explain. Louise, I promise, I'll have everything dry cleaned. The rug will be shampooed."

Gorgeous gasped. "It's the waitress again. She's in Louise's house, smoking marijuana! Detective Perez is on the way and we could all be arrested."

"It's sage," Signe assured, holding out her hand, stop-sign fashion. "Don't worry, Louise, it's only sage."

Sensing his advantage, James shooed everyone out, just as Signe had the smoke, then he leaned against the closed door and called over the blaring siren, "What's going on in here, Signe?"

Somehow, she didn't think he'd believe her if she lied and said she smoked cigarettes but had been trying to hide the fact from him. Worse, seeing him standing so close, just across the room, she could scarcely stop herself from running into his arms. He, of course, was no longer under her spell, but that didn't mean her own feelings had changed. She wanted those strong arms circling around her back again, and she wanted to make love to him.

Tears stung eyes she'd nearly shut against the smoke. Had she really cast a spell to ensure he'd never love her? She was even more miserable now than she'd been before!

That must mean she loved him, she decided. Maybe it had started with a witch's spell, but the lovemaking in his cabin...that had been real, right? So were the emotions she'd felt when he'd followed her into the city to return her ring, not to mention how they'd amused each other, drizzling chocolate over each other's bodies and slowly licking it off....

She was powerless to stop the tear that rolled down her cheek, but she quickly swiped it away. She'd made such a mess of everything. "How could everything we did be based in a lie," she whispered miserably.

11

"It's not, sweetheart," James assured quickly, striding across the room toward where she stood at the window, pausing under the sprinkler to hit the switch in the ceiling mechanism. Everything went silent in the absence of the hissing water and piercing alarm. And then he heard the rain again. "Dammit, Signe—" he began, his voice sounding overly loud.

"Don't you dare curse me," she returned before he could finish his sentence. "I haven't done anything wrong, James," she said.

He'd stilled his steps under the sprinkler, vaguely aware that a mess of stuff lay on the floor. "I tried to call you all week, and when you refused to answer your phone—"

"I had good reasons for not answering."

"What?"

"Self-protection."

"You know I'd never hurt you."

She straightened her shoulders, clearly trying to restore her self-respect, since she'd nearly burned down his sister's house and was drenched to the bone. "You already have by lying to me."

Okay. Maybe he hadn't told the whole truth, but was that really the same as a lie? "Did you really

think I was using you or something? That I didn't
want you to think I was a Garrity?"

"You didn't. You would have told me."

He shrugged, changing tack. "I've tried to talk to
you. I came by your place."

"Really?"

As if she didn't know. From the other side of the
peephole, he'd been staring directly at one of her
eyes, which had been pressed to the hole. The rejection had been a new experience. Most of his life, especially when women knew he was a Garrity, a
phone call or flowers would do the trick, but Signe
was different. Which was why he needed her so
much. He started toward the window again.

"Don't come any nearer," she said stoically.

Compromising by slowing, rather than halting his
steps, he dragged a frustrated hand through whatever the salon had left of his hair. It wasn't much. Just
a few strands. Almost a crew cut. And he'd done all
that for her! The haircut. The suit. The flowers. The
romantic fires in the fireplace. Maybe the worst thing
was that he hadn't much minded. He'd even enjoyed
the fact that it had given his mother pleasure. He'd totally rethought his confirmed bachelor status. "Why
are you so mad at me? This isn't really about my family name. It can't be."

"Lying's terrible no matter who you are," she said,
looking oddly nervous. "And you acted as if you
needed a makeover. You came to Diane's for the pur-
pose of getting to know me, and—"

"I never lied about that."

"You're not really a park ranger."

"Sure I am."

"Anyway, that's not the point."

"What is?"

"That you let me..."

His heart soared unexpectedly as her voice trailed off.

Looking at her stricken expression, he was sure she'd been about to say "let me fall in love with you," but she didn't feel comfortable uttering the words, because she felt it had been under false pretenses. "Let you care about me?"

"I'd say you're presumptuous," she muttered. "But okay. I admit it. I started to care about you."

The pain in her dark eyes said she felt even more. "You care for me, even though you thought you were too good for me?"

"I don't think that. You know it. We've had that argument so many times I'm not even going there."

At least they were talking. He strode toward her, stopping in front of her, and said, "No matter how it happened, I'm glad for everything. We wound up in bed, and then..."

Kismet. He'd been hoping that they could talk today, and he'd brought a peace offering, a gift he knew she'd love. He couldn't wait to see her face light up when she opened the gift box, and all day he'd been hoping it would turn out to be one of those small gestures that would be the exact right thing.

"You didn't need a makeover, but you let me believe you did, and you acted as if you didn't know anything about art, too."

"I don't," he defended.

Reaching a hand upward, she brushed droplets from her face and stared at him, her gaze strangely curious now, although he had no idea why. "Just because everybody else in my family is into art, doesn't mean I am, Signe. And yeah," he admitted, "you're right. They've dragged me to galleries ever since I can remember. Openings. Shows. But the only time I've ever really enjoyed those things was when I was with you."

Her eyes were narrowing, searching his nervously. "Why don't I believe you?"

"Fear?"

She arched an incredulous brow, once more pushing the wet hair away from her face. "Of?"

"Me. My family. Wealth." He shrugged. "But we don't have to live like that."

Her lips parted, as if she meant to contradict him, but then she clamped her mouth shut. His gaze roved over her face, and only now did he realize he'd half feared he'd never see her again. His heart pulled as he looked at what the sprinkler had done to her face, smudging eye makeup she didn't usually wear, but which she'd put on for his mother. He thought to offer the tail of his shirt and wipe away the mascara, but he knew this wasn't the moment.

"Maybe I was afraid," she finally said, then cryptically added, "but it doesn't matter now."

He couldn't help but inch closer, crossing an invisible magic line she'd drawn in the air. As soon as he had, he knew it was simply too difficult to be this close, at least when she wasn't loving him. He needed her in his arms again, with her mouth locked to his, their hips cradling, and the heat rising between them, smoking just like this room. Lifting an arm, he placed it above her head on the window frame, fighting the urge to kiss her. "The hell I didn't need that make-over," he suddenly muttered.

"How could you? You're a Garrity."

"Sure," he agreed, but what she'd really made over was his heart. "The black sheep Garrity. With hair down to my shoulders and a job as a park ranger."

"Which is your choice."

"You're right about that, Signe. And the truth is, if my brother ever really screws up, the silent agreement I have with my father—" He paused, feeling winded from how her enticing scent was rising to his nostrils. "Is that I'll step in, clean up my act and run the business. You might as well know. I've got a degree in ecology as well as an MBA. Harvard both." Pausing once more, he offered a wry chuckle. "Mostly because my father's a Yale man. Choosing another school was my first big act of rebellion."

He flashed her what under other circumstances might have been a smile. "The hair came later," he continued. "Then the job as a park ranger. I really do want to write my novel, too. If I ever decided to get a white-collar job, I'd probably look in the field of environmental conservation." He sighed. "Anyway, I don't understand why this affects how you feel about me."

"It affects everything! You were dishonest about who you are and where you came from. Everything we have is built on lies. But it's not just that. It's worse. It's not just you, and what you did. It's me, too. You've got to understand that I—"

How could this be worse? He was crazy with wanting her, sure she was going to leave him, just as he was thoroughly entranced by her dark eyes, which were dancing with anger. He decided he liked exactly what he'd known his mother would about her—her backbone. Not many women would walk away from a Garrity who was so clearly smitten with her. "Can you at least admit we have something?" His voice lowered. "Remember how we were kissing, outside the library..." They were ready to promise their hearts before his father had arrived, blown his cover and ruined everything.

"Sure. Or I thought we did. But you have to know what I—"

Unable to believe the seeming apology mixed with anger over the lie *he'd* told, he said, "I omitted the truth." He couldn't let her take any of the blame for this. "Aren't you curious about why?"

His eyes riveted on the pulse visibly racing in her throat as she swallowed. "Are you sure you really care about me?"

This was a shift. "Yeah."

She was peering at him through suspicious eyes. "I mean, right now? At this very minute."

What was she driving at? "Yeah," he returned, but the way she was looking at him, he was starting to doubt himself.

She looked puzzled. "You're *sure?*"

"What—"

"You really feel something?"

"Yes."

Encouraged by the fact that she was at least curious about how he felt, he murmured, "Here," and raised the tail of his shirt to her damp cheek. "You've got makeup all over your face."

She exhaled a sexy sigh of protest. She still looked stricken, but she dutifully tilted back her head and let him wipe away the smudges. He took his time. He'd missed being able to touch her like this. He hadn't left Manhattan since he'd last seen her because he'd felt compelled to stay as close to her as possible. He'd felt that if he left the island, he might lose his window of opportunity and never see her again.

"There." As he drew away his hand, it felt so bereft that he slid a thumb upward on her neck and lifted her chin, to better look into her eyes. His voice husky, he repeated, "Don't you want to know why I didn't tell you?"

She looked thoroughly undecided. As if she'd rather be anywhere but standing in front of him with his finger now skating across the skin of her cheek, one of his sandals edging between her two parted feet and his lips inching to within a breath of hers. She asked, "Why?"

Leaning back a fraction, he shrugged, his warring emotions making his voice tense. "You can't know what it's like to be a Garrity," he began. "How many women come on to you. How many dig into each other, behind your back, pulling catty maneuvers, so you'll date them. And all the while, if they really searched their souls and asked themselves the truth, they'd realize they don't even like you, not really.

· "In college, there were lots of women like that," he
continued. "George ate it up. That's when he got the
nickname Gorgeous. He didn't care about their motivations. Or who knows? Maybe my brother didn't
understand them any more than he seems to understand his own."

His eyes found hers again, the gaze penetrating. "I
watched you at dinner. And you were watching them
all, Signe. Taking in the show. You saw how they all
go at one another, the games they play. And it's all
about Dad. He sits in the background, hardly saying
a word, but everyone's trying to impress him. And
you know why?"

She was staring at him, wide-eyed, as if whatever
he was saying was taking this in a direction she
hadn't anticipated. When she shook her head, he
nearly whispered the words, "Money. The Garrity
fortune. Everybody wants to make sure they get a fair
share." Stroking a finger down her cheek, he sighed
in frustration.

"You ought to see it," he continued. "Every time
there's a family fight, people whisper about who's being cut out of his will. Or what the offending party
will need to do to get back into Dad's good graces.
Honestly, Signe, I can't stand it. No more than I can
stand the conversations about which artworks should
be donated to which galleries after we all die.

"In the Garrity family," he finished, "there's too
much history. I think that cut many of us off from the
present. And that's where I want to live. The present.
About the women..."

His eyes raked down over her face, taking in lovely

eyes that were so hard to read right now. Surely, they could return to the way they were, he thought, to the blissful week of sex they'd shared before his damn family got in the way.

Her voice sounded faint. "The women?"

"In college, I used to go off campus, down to the local bars. I'd dress down. Throw on some old jeans and a T-shirt. Just go for a beer. You know, no dart games with my brother's frat friends. No pressures. And when girls flirted with me, I started lying about my name. I'd introduce myself as Joe Smith. Or Kevin Jones. That was a name I used a lot. I got a taste of what it felt like to be...myself, I guess. That's when I realized I wanted out of the Garrity rat race." He peered at her carefully, not wanting her to misunderstand. "I accept who I am," he assured her. "I know where I come from, what it means. But I want more."

"You want more than to be a Garrity?"

He nodded. "I want my own life."

"And that's why you didn't tell me the whole truth?"

She still didn't understand. Swiftly cupping her face, he stared deep into her eyes. "Don't you see, Signe? It's like years ago, back in those college bars. Your not knowing who I was made everything perfect for us. Made what we have so much more real. I wasn't trying to fool you, just let you get to know the real me, without all the family baggage."

He didn't understand this at all. The more he spoke, the more horrified she looked. Her eyes were filling with so much pain he simply couldn't bear it. "Damn," he suddenly cursed again, and when she didn't immediately answer, he added, "You really don't know what you've done to me, Signe."

Her eyes were piercing deeply into his. "That's the problem, James," she said, her voice sounding strained, its soft murmur barely more than a rasp. "I'm afraid I do."

Her eyes slid from his, over his shoulder, and he turned to follow her gaze, finding himself squinting into the floor. The smoke had cleared, and he could make out a magic circle on the floor formed by strands of straw. Inside was a bell, candle and some bundled herbs, which he supposed had been the source of the smoke, as well as a thick black book, up-turned so that it was spine out. Embossed on the cover in gold leaf were the words: *Witch's Source Book.*

Just as he headed toward it, wondering what on earth she'd been up to, she whispered in a voice laced with misery, "I can explain everything."

"What do you have to explain?"

"You no longer care about me," she whispered cryptically, sounding wistful and sad, her throat hoarse with emotion. "You just think you do. It may even *feel* as if you do. At least for a few more minutes. But it's probably just some sort of residual effect...."

What was she talking about? Leaning, he lifted the book from the floor. As he did, a sheet of paper fluttered from the pages, and he recognized the writing as hers. Catching the note before it hit the floor, he then turned his attention to a marginal notation that read, "Use this on James."

As his eyes followed the arrow to a spell, he muttered, "Yeah, you'd better explain." And yet he wasn't sure he wanted to hear whatever she had to say. His lips parted in surprise as he read, and then he was simply fighting to tamp down his anger. He murmured:

"Oh, ye spirits do hear me
In a crystal ball do see
An eve of sexy revelry
With a man I call Garrity
And if we should be good in bed...

So, she'd known he was a Garrity all along. He paused, catching his breath. Well, they'd been good in bed, too. So, he guessed she figured the spell had worked. Anytime he thought about thrusting deep inside her, his whole body would start to burn as if it was on fire. Dammit, was this really the end of their affair? Would he ever forget her? How could he ever forgive her deception? No wonder she'd looked so guilty. He continued:

"...if we should be good in bed
I beseech ye, we should wed
And now that this has all been said
I give this handkerchief of red

"I told you I cast a spell..." she murmured.

When had she gotten hold of one of his handkerchiefs? She'd have had to dig deep in his drawers. While it was true his mother put them in his stocking each Christmas, James rarely carried them. His eyes shifted from the paper to the spell in the book once more. His breath caught as he silently read it, unable to believe she'd done it.

Reverse the magic. Forget the logic.

Not only had she known he was a Garrity, once he'd fallen for her, she'd turned around and reversed the spell. He lifted his eyes to hers, his heart thudding. "You wanted to reverse it?" he muttered, barely able to believe their affair had meant so little to her. "To erase our chemistry? To let the magic fade?"

She nodded solemnly.

Obviously, she didn't even feel bad about rejecting him this way. Not that he believed in witchcraft in the least. Never had, never would. Oh, he'd felt so beguiled he'd almost believed he'd been bewitched the first few times they were together, and...well, maybe he still did, but only in the sense that what they'd shared was a magic unto itself.

"That was the lie I was talking about," she managed to say.

It was impossible to subdue his anger. It was like a wound right now, eating him up from the inside out. "I should have known. You targeted me, didn't you?"

How could she have done it? She'd seemed so innocent. "You knew I was a Garrity all along," he persisted in soft accusation as he moved toward her. Lips that, moments ago, had wanted only to kiss her now parted in astonishment, and his eyes narrowed as if he'd never seen her before. And he guessed he hadn't. Not for the deceptive woman she really was. "Oh, you're good," he said.

"No!" she cried, her jaw going slack. "You've got it all wrong!"

"Do I?" he asked rhetorically, stepping closer, his voice laced with barely suppressed emotion. As he stopped in front of her, she slunk against the windowsill, and this time, he completely understood her desire to escape. He didn't blame her. "You looked so sweet. So innocent. So sincere."

"I am," she claimed.

"Really?" he chided, so close to her now that he knew she was feeling the heat of his breath on her lips. "And to think I've felt guilty since that night at Gilda's," he muttered, trying to conceal his hurt.

"Yeah," he continued, feeling disgusted with himself. "I felt so bad about not telling you the truth." Now, given her deception, he wanted to punish her for every lonely moment he'd spent lying in bed, thinking about her, torturing himself as he recalled each nuance of their lovemaking. Each night, he'd lain in the dark, remembering her until he was hot, sweating and hard, the sheets damp beneath him. He'd touched himself, too. Stroked himself and pretended they were really her fingers on his flesh. The little witch sure knew how to put a spell on a man. "I thought you really liked me."

She gasped. "I do like—"

"Even believed you might be falling in love with—"

"I was—"

"And the way we were in bed. I thought it was the hottest, sexiest, most mind-blowing—"

"It was! It was! But it was only because of the

spell!" she insisted. "It wasn't *real,* James. It could never last. And I'd never know what would have happened if we'd met in, uh, a more natural way."

He'd barely heard her words. "And now, after you made me feel so guilty, it turns out you're the one who lied to me."

She shook her head adamantly. "No!"

"You knew I was a Garrity all along," he repeated dully.

"I thought you were a park ranger and, well, I guess you really are. But you see—"

Her words were catching up to him now. Had she really said she'd been falling in love with him?

Before he could ask, he realized the stricken look had returned to her face. As her skin paled, her dark eyes started looking stark against her cheeks, and as he watched the transformation, he silently damned himself. Whatever was happening, nothing could stop how much he wanted her. A part of him didn't even want explanations for her duplicity. He wanted to open the spell book, read every piece of magic pertaining to love and burn that weird smoke until he was sure she belonged to him forever.

"What you don't understand," she whispered, her voice shaking so much that he could barely make out what she was saying. "I didn't cast a spell for you, James."

"The spell said 'an eve of sexy revelry with the man I call Garrity.' If not me, who?"

"Uh...Gorgeous."

He nearly choked. "I guess that would explain the bit with the handkerchief," he said. His brother never would be caught without one. His eyes widened, then he mouthed the words, "My brother?"

When spots of color rose on her cheeks, James could hardly say he blamed her for being embarrassed. No one in their right mind would cast a spell on Gorgeous, not unless they were strictly interested in money. Or unless they weren't exceptionally bright and, like Christine, didn't mind spending two years of female labor to get James's brother to propose. He could only stare at Signe. It was definitely the wrong time to remember how much he'd loved plundering that sweet mouth and making her moan for some shared heat.

"Gorgeous?" he muttered.

"I didn't really know him," she defended.

"And that's supposed to be better?" He shook his head, wanting the truth, and yet not wanting it. "What were you...?"

"After?"

He forced himself to nod.

She edged away as if she might bolt and run, and when he put out a hand to stop her, not about to let her go, she crossed her arms over her breasts. The movement hardly calmed his pulse rate. The blouse she wore under a tan blazer had gotten soaked, and he was staring through the transparent fabric to the lace bra beneath. "The first night," he said, his words scarcely discernible, "you thought I was..."

Gorgeous? Neither of them could say the word again. "Not really," she said quickly. "When you...touched me, I guess all thoughts of him left my mind. Actually, after that, I didn't think about him again. Not once. It was as if I'd never had a crush on him at all. But don't you see..."

"See what?"

"That's the problem! The spell was accidently cast on you!"

James's eyes implored her, but he was sure nothing she'd say at this point could remedy the situation, even though he kept hoping she'd burst out laughing. Yes, somehow, this would all turn out to be a big joke. A hoax. Something they'd still be laughing about later, when they were hitting the proverbial sheets. When her tongue darted nervously out, to lick her lips, he became just that much more aware of how her proximity was sending waves of lust through his system.

"Your brother used to come to the Met," she began. That was a known fact. "On his lunch hour."

He could almost see the wheels turning in her devious mind as she tried to decide what to say next. "And he'd flirt with me." Quickly, she added, "that was before he married Christine." Sighing, she changed her mind, and said, "Well, maybe it wouldn't have mattered. I mean, at dinner, he didn't even remember me...."

At this point, James felt almost struck catatonic. He was just watching that tasty mouth move, while, with every word, she dug herself in deeper. "And?"

"You're not even trying to listen," she murmured miserably, "so I guessed it must have really worked."

He squinted. "What must have worked?"

She stared at him as if he were an idiot. "The reversal spell on you." She paused. "I mean, the original spell was on him, but then it worked on you, you see, so I had to do something, so that you *wouldn't* be deceived. Because of the spell, nothing between us was real...."

He was unable to take all this in. He was still a number of pages back. "You had a crush on my brother?" How could he respect a woman who'd been the least bit attracted to Gorgeous?

"*Had*," Signe said significantly.

"You don't now?"

"Of course not!"

She sounded mortified, which was to her credit. "Nothing against your brother," she added, "but...well, he seemed charming in the Met. And he'd always stop for coffee and flirt. And he is good-looking."

James nodded, able to admit that much.

"He was at the Halloween party, where I was serving drinks," she continued, "the night your uncle Harold's statue was stolen...." She stared hard into his eyes, as if she was looking for evidence that he wasn't still bewitched, then continued thoughtfully, "Yes...your brother was there the night the statue went missing. Anyway," she finished on a sigh. "He seemed wealthy, charming and he was..."

The bane of James's existence. "A Garrity."

Her eyes slid away from his, and when she spoke, her words sounded strangled. "Yes. Casting the spell was just a joke, though. My girlfriends and I were headed up to the Catskills for the wiccan retreat. I didn't really know your brother, and I didn't think he'd turn up..."

"In your cabin?"

"In my bed."

"*My* bed," he corrected her.

Still looking at her, wondering where to go from here, he exhaled slowly. Just as he did, a motor sounded. Looking relieved for the distraction, Signe turned toward the sound. Glancing over her shoulder, James peered through rain that had tempered to a drizzle and saw a black sedan coming up the driveway. Even from here, he could see two passengers.

"Perez and Styles," she said. "They must have driven up from the city together."

As soon as the words were out, she gasped, and suddenly thrust her upper body out the window, pushing out the screen. James didn't have time to process what she was doing. Swiftly grabbing her waist, he yanked, trying to haul her inside, but she fought, holding on to the window frame while he muttered, "Get back in here, Signe. It's raining."

"I'm already wet," she growled.

She slapped his hands away, and if he wasn't so mad, he might not have minded. Feeling her squirming against him for the first time in days made heat flood his groin, which was pressed hard to her backside. When his hand touched the bare skin of her rib cage, he wanted to draw her closer, forget their argument and hold her tightly against him. Maybe he'd never let go.

"Stop!" she shouted. "You two stop!" Under her breath, she muttered, "I recognize them. I saw them that night."

"Who?" He was still trying to pull her inside. "What night?"

Styles and Perez were coming down the driveway, so she couldn't be yelling at them. Tucking a hand down the waistband of her skirt, James got a good grip and tugged, and while she didn't dislodge from the window, he gained some visibility, enough to see that she was yelling at his nephews.

"Don't move! You'd better stay right there!" Sounding livid, she said, "Their names are Steven and Charles, right?"

James nodded, wondering if this was a ploy to derail their argument. He wanted to hash out their differences, come up with some understanding about the spell she'd cast on him....

Outside, the boys were running, their shoes sliding in the wet grass. Before he could protest, Signe whirled in his arms, batting away his hands. Every bit of blessed heat he'd felt just a minute ago, crushed against his groin, was now searing down his entire front side. Her two hands landed on his shoulders and she pushed him away. "Get out of my way, James," she demanded, her eyes flashing with temper right before she ran past him.

Determined to save his own breath, he decided to at least look out the window before he followed her, to see what the ruckus was about. Detective Perez and Edmond Styles were still heading up the driveway, and James's nephews were running toward the beach beneath a copse of trees and foliage that lined the circular drive, trying to stay out of the drizzle. From the back the boys looked almost alike. Although Charles was eleven and Steven was thirteen, they were roughly the same height; they'd changed for tea, and were wearing navy slacks and blazers. Ties that James thought they were too young to wear were blowing over their shoulders as they ran. They were moving at a clip.

So was Signe.

She shot from the front veranda like a rocket, her hair dripping, her clothes suctioned against her skin, one of her shoes—which she didn't stop to retrieve— flying off as she ran. "Hold it!" she shrieked. "Stop right there!"

Something was in Steven's hand. Charles was running a pace behind, flailing to grab an item that was dark in color and about a foot long. James squinted. And then he inhaled sharply. "Well, I'll be," he muttered.

It was the missing statue of Eros.

"I SAID STOP!" SIGNE SHOUTED. She glanced to where James had caught up, running beside her, but she didn't slow down. She was flying, her head down, fists pumping. Drizzle pelted her face, and her teeth chattered as her own momentum brought wind against her drenched clothes. "They've got the statue of Eros," she said on a pant, her mind reeling from their argument, her eyes riveted on the boys diving over a hill where grass turned into sand dunes.

"I know." James barely sounded winded. "I saw it."

Her side was splitting, her lungs about to burst, but she pushed herself harder, feeling the ground give under her stocking feet and wishing she hadn't lost a shoe. She'd kicked off the other, finding it easier to run without both. Looking over her shoulder, she saw Detective Perez and Edmond Styles getting out of the sedan and giving chase. Had they seen the statue, also? From the car?

"The kids are too fast!"

"Not for me." When James bounded in front of her, she realized he'd only slowed to keep pace with her, and her heart ached. He was so graceful, the tails of his white shirt blowing behind him like sails to expose the glossy tanned skin of his back. Embarrassed heat flooded her. Yes...as soon as she got the statue, she could hop in the car and get out of here. She wouldn't even need to have tea with Jacqueline Garrity, now that Eros was found.

As James vanished over the hill, she sped up, glad when physical exertion heightened her focus, crowding out her confusion. She'd felt mortified upstairs. James had caught her trolling for a rich husband. It hardly mattered that casting the spells had been a lark between friends. Now that she'd seen Gorgeous in his own milieu, she understood exactly why his own brother had stared at her like that.

James's family had caught her practicing witchcraft, too, and even thought she'd been smoking marijuana. She simply couldn't face them after nearly burning down one of Louise Amherst's bedrooms. The final injury had been the look on James's face when he'd read the spell reversal. Pain knifed through her now. He'd looked hurt, but what else could she have done? Previously, she hadn't really believed in the craft, but the spell had worked. Winding up bed with James had been too much of a coincidence. And while the wrong bed had turned out to be the right bed, was it really? Why couldn't he see that she'd had no choice but to revoke their...love.

And it was love, wasn't it? She dipped over the hill now, her feet ploughing into sand. James was confronting the boys. His hands were on his hips; Steven was still holding the statue, and both boys were doubled over, gasping for breath.

"Give that to me," she demanded breathlessly

when she reached them, bypassing James and wrenching the statue from his nephew Steven's hand. As soon as her hand closed securely around the artifact, relief flooded her. She, too, doubled, pressing her hand to the pain in her side, her throat feeling raw as she sucked down harsh breaths. Avoiding James's gaze, she felt the weight of the object in her hands. It was definitely Eros.

"Is that what we think it is?" Detective Perez called.

Glancing over her shoulder, she watched him and Edmond Styles bolt into the dunes. Gorgeous, Harold, Jacqueline and Louise followed.

"I wanted to give it back," Steven began. "But Charles wouldn't let me!"

"You took it!" countered the younger boy. His eyes darted wildly around the circle of adults. "You turned off the alarm, Steven." Charles's eyes implored Louise. "He did, Mom."

"I was going to give it back!"

"I saw them at the Halloween party," Signe interjected, her eyes shifting between Styles and Perez. "They were there...." With Gorgeous, she realized now. He must have brought them to the party. "When I looked out the window, I recognized them. I didn't know they were related to you...."

"They're my sons," said Louise. "And they've got some explaining to do."

"He thought it was going to make him more potent," charged Charles. "He made me swear not to tell, but I knew the statue was Uncle Harold's."

All eyes turned to Steven. He looked as mortified

as Signe felt over the encounter with James. She couldn't bear to face him. What must he think of her? What kind of a woman cast a spell to have sex with a man? Much less a jerk like Gorgeous? And then, when she landed the wrong brother, what kind of woman would almost burn down a house in an effort to correct the situation? Thunder clapped. As she looked up, lightning flashed, striking where the waves had turned dangerously dark and choppy. She turned her attention to the boys again.

"I am *so* potent," a horrified Steven was defending.

"Then why did you steal the potency statue?" challenged his brother, shaking with anger. Clearly, he'd been threatened with bodily death if he returned the missing artifact. "I was chasing him," the younger boy assured them. "I was trying to get it back. I didn't know what to do. We're not supposed to be tattletales, but he stole it, to get some girl."

The thirteen-year-old's face was almost as bright as the scarlet stripes in a patriotic American-flag-inspired tie that he wore with his blue suit. "Don't listen to Charles. I thought…"

"That this girl at school, Alice Pennington, would go out with him if he had the statue," explained Charles victoriously.

"Alice Pennington?" asked Louise.

For the next few minutes, Steven rambled about a girl he'd met. "She liked me at the beginning of the school year," he explained. "Then she started talking to another guy. Not that I care," he quickly added. "She's just some stupid girl, but I thought…"

"The statue's been under his bed," announced

Charles. "I knew it was somewhere, and I just found it. I was bringing it downstairs to show you, Mom, but he got it away from me, and—"

"I got blamed for the theft," Signe interjected.

Both boys stared at her, then Charles said, "You were working at the party."

"Uncle Gorgeous was talking to you when...uh... the alarm switch got turned off," said Steven.

James aside, most of the Garrity males seemed to have a truly annoying short-term memory deficit when it came to the wait staff. "Yes. I was."

"Sorry," Charles murmured.

"I hope you didn't get into trouble," added Steven graciously.

"I lost my job."

"Oh, that's just silliness!" Jacqueline spoke, looking as calm, cool and collected as royalty in an ivory knit dress and matching shawl. She was the only one who'd bothered with an umbrella, and given its size, everyone present could have fit beneath it. "After all, Signe's such a good friend of ours—"

Edmond Styles was wringing his hands. "I had no idea, Signe. I mean—er—Ms. Sargent. You should have let me know you were a personal friend of the Garritys. I hope you'll forgive this misunderstanding."

For a fleeting second, Signe's eyes met James's. Everything inside her clenched. In this light, his eyes were a glowing amber color, warm perhaps, but also unreadable. Suddenly, she ached for the loving feel of his embrace, and the surge of connection that sex with him had brought. She forced herself to turn away. "Don't worry," she managed to say to Edmond Styles, her voice strangled with emotion, tears pressuring her eyelids, making them burn. "We're not really close," she said. "We're just recently acquainted, in fact."

Moving forward, she held out the statue to the two men. "Here. One of you had better take this."

"That would be me," said Detective Perez, surveying her through piercing black eyes as he took Eros, the thumb and forefinger of his free hand catching the end of his mustache and pulling distractedly. "I'll make sure it's safely returned to the museum." He took in her bedraggled state. "I underestimated you, Ms. Sargent. Thank you for recovering the statue."

"You were right," she felt compelled to concede in a voice that only he could hear, since she really hadn't done as much as he was crediting her for. "The cats were my girlfriends."

The tips of the mustache lifted in a smile. "I thought so."

"Jolly good," agreed Harold excitedly. When she felt a pawlike hand clamp down on her shoulder, Signe felt as if she were a long-lost sports chum of Harold Garrity's from Harvard. "Really," he commended. "Good show. That night at Gilda's, who would have suspected you were working undercover?"

Under the covers would have been more like it, but it would take too long to divest this group of their illusions about her role, Signe decided. She certainly didn't want to explain that if she hadn't cast a spell on

Gorgeous, hoping to sleep with him, maybe none of this would have happened.

Edmond Styles was cringing. "We'll see you on Monday?" He paused nervously. "That would, of course, be in the new position you were offered in archives. Of course, if such a position isn't really suitable..."

She didn't like that he felt railroaded. However, she had worked hard to create the opportunity for herself at the Met, and she had fulfilled her responsibilities to the museum on Halloween night. "Archives is just wonderful," she assured him warmly. "A dream come true, Mr. Styles. I look forward to working with you again."

He looked tremendously relieved. "Monday, then."

"Now, let's all have tea," said Jacqueline reasonably.

"Really, Ms. Garrity—" Signe extended her hand and shook James's mother's. "It's been wonderful to meet you, but I need to get back to the city. I hope you'll understand. I'm just glad the statue has been recovered."

Jacqueline looked disappointed. "I wish you'd stay." She paused delicately. "And visit with James, but if you must..."

"I must," assured Signe. Given how angry and hurt James had looked upstairs, she knew she had to leave. She wouldn't be welcome here. After what she'd done, how could he so much as look at her? Trying to ignore the unbearable constriction of her throat, she turned around to face James, determined to meet his gaze and say a quiet, simple "goodbye."

But he was gone.

TWENTY MINUTES LATER, Signe had tossed her belongings into the front seat and was gripping the wheel of the compact. Her driving had been bad enough when the weather was clear, but now rain was coming down. She hunched her shoulders, peering through the deluge, and fumbled with gadgets, hoping to make the wipers go faster. "There," she murmured.

Not that she felt better. After returning to the house, she hadn't seen James. And secretly, hadn't she been hoping he'd confront her and beg her to stay?

It was wishful thinking. Childish, given how he must feel about her now, but she'd wanted him to come into the bedroom, his eyes as stormy as the dark sky, and wrap his arms around her, rip off her wet clothes and briskly dry her before they made love. Instead, she'd gathered her things quickly and fled, still feeling mortified. She hadn't even bothered to change clothes.

Now she was freezing. And lost. She'd just passed a fork in the road, one she realized was probably pointing toward the beach rather than the city, but there was no place to turn around. Besides, maybe she was wrong. She was also beginning to suspect that the car was malfunctioning. She didn't know anything about cars—she counted herself lucky to be driving with any dexterity whatsoever—but she kept hearing a strange squeal. Was it the engine? Or maybe something less serious? Such as the heater, which she'd turned on high?

As water sloshed across the windshield, she shivered, wishing tears weren't pushing at her eyes. She wasn't going to cry over a man, not even a Garrity, especially since it was she who'd botched things so badly. And whatever happened, she was Signe Sargent, woman of Manhattan, lone child of the Minneapolis Sargents who would always love her, no matter how much of a fool she'd just made of herself. She could hang on to that.

Her week with James had been pure magic, though. A spell. A fantasy. And now it was over. *Just be happy for the blissful interlude.* The days strolling around Manhattan, the sultry nights between the sheets. Blinking rapidly, she told herself that the panicked tears threatening to fall were only a response to the fact that she was lost. She wanted to get away from this enclave where he'd hidden himself....

A road sign loomed ahead. Brushing her cheek with the back of her hand before using it to swipe away fog on the glass, she told herself that the dampness on her face wasn't tears, but rain. Yes, the stupid rain was everywhere. Impeding her progress. Making it impossible to get home. Or to read the sign.

And the car was going to die. The squeal was worse. She'd be stuck and have to call a tow service on her cell. Yes, she could see herself, standing in the road, wetter and colder than she already was. While her car was being repaired, she'd be stuck in the Hamptons, and no hotel would have vacancies. She'd have to call Louise and return....

Realizing she was getting hysterical, she tried not to focus on the squealing, or on the fact that she'd probably never see James again, and felt a flood of relief when she did manage to read the sign. Unfortunately, it showed an arrow, pointed in the direction she was headed. It was printed with one word: Beach.

Definitely not a good sign.

She was headed away from the city, but up ahead, a structure loomed from the gloom. A tourist's information office would be too much to ask for, especially since she was sure that every inch of beach within miles was private. "Please stop," she whispered to the infernal squealing, then added, "A gazebo."

Through a haze of rain, she could make out a parking area. Good. She could stop. Regroup. Maybe change into dry clothes in the car, if no one was around. Or were they? Squinting, she thought she saw someone in the gazebo. Or was it a trick of the light?

Hopefully, it was a person. And he or she could tell her how to get back to the city. As she stopped in the lot, flashes of lightning angled through a turbulent sky, piercing the crashing waves. A clap of thunder sounded, and it was brutal, the kind of unforgiving, scary thunder that had driven her into her parents' bedroom at night when she was a kid.

Someone was in the gazebo! "Thank you," she whispered. She drove as close as she could get, then turned off the motor before fear claimed her. What if the person was some weirdo? She grabbed the cell but figured she was just being paranoid. New York life was affecting her faith in human kindness. Taking a deep breath, she turned to the back seat, hoping to find an umbrella left by a previous car rental customer.

A box.

It was white, maybe a foot square in size and sitting in the center of the back seat. She'd been in a rush to leave, then so focused on driving that she hadn't noticed. Quickly she reached forward to pull it into the front seat.

The lid tumbled off, and when she looked inside, tears fell in earnest. A yellow, black-striped Bengal kitten, no doubt left by James, was huddled on a towel. It stared up at her, its amber eyes looking positively wounded, as if Signe had been its only hope, but had now miserably failed. Yes, it was as if Signe was the meanest person alive....

"That's where the squeal was coming from. Oh, you poor little thing," Signe crooned, her chin trembling, a tear sliding down her cheek, her hand gingerly scooping up the infuriated, quivering ball of fur. Signe senselessly murmured, whispered and kissed the kitten—until it ceased yowling and began to arch its back and lift its tiny tail in pleasure, raising its face, so that Signe could slip the tip of a finger beneath and scratch under its chin.

James had done this for her. He must have brought the kitty to the Hamptons as a make-up gift. Despite what had happened and his realizations concerning the spell reversal, he'd still left the kitten for her....

"Magic," she whispered, her eyes stinging. "That's what I'll call you." Surely this meant James still cared for her, that he'd forgive her. He'd left Magic for her to find, a pet who'd be there for her, even when he was gone. Didn't he understand that Signe hadn't really wanted to leave? Not deep down? It was up to him to forgive her! She was the one in the wrong. She'd been such a jerk.

She peered through the murky windshield. Through sprays of rain she could see the figure in the gazebo. She was sure it was a man, but it was hard to tell. Surely the person could tell her how to get back to...

The Garritys.

Wasn't that where she needed to go? Staring down at the kitten in her palm, she decided she simply couldn't go back to the city. James leaving her this bundle of joy must be a sign.

"Wait right here," she whispered, and even though the kitten released a long, plaintive series of meows as it was resituated in the box, Signe wasn't about to be swayed. "I have to get out for a minute," she explained, stroking the kitten's head, "and get directions. But I'll be right back. I promise."

With that, she opened the car door and plunged into the rain, gripping the loose ends of her wet jacket against her chest and squinting, blinking water from her eyes as she ran for the gazebo. "Excuse me," she shouted as she reached the structure, peering through the curtain of gray rain that fell like a sheet from the gutters, so that she couldn't see inside. "Excuse me—" Closer now, she could see that it probably was a man inside. "Sir, I need some directions. Maybe you could help me."

With a heave of relief, she ran up the stairs, ducking under the curtain of rain. "Sir, I—"

Very slowly, James Garrity began to turn around. Her breath stilled. Tears stung her eyes. This was the last thing she expected. It really was pure magic this time, and yet she'd never even cast a spell. He'd been leaning forward, his hands closed over the railing, staring at the sea. Stunned, she waited until he was fully facing her, then she simply said, "James."

"I thought you left."

She could scarcely believe he was really here. "I did. I found the kitten."

"You like it?"

"Oh, yes!" He had no idea how much. What had he said? *You have no idea what you've done to me, Signe.* Well, she felt the same way. Moving toward him, she said, "After I found the kitten, I was going to turn around and go back to Louise's, but I'd gotten lost and needed directions—"

He simply grabbed her and pulled her into his embrace. Her cheek melted against his chest. Suddenly, she wasn't the least bit cold any longer. The man seemed to wrap around her not once, but ten times. His voice was hoarse above the sheet of rain falling all around them. "You don't need directions. You're right where you're supposed to be, Signe."

In my arms. Her mind couldn't catch up. He'd been at the house only moments ago. "How did you get here?"

"Took a shortcut in my Jeep."

She hadn't seen another car, but then, she hadn't really looked. "What are you doing here?"

"I come here to think. My father built this gazebo years ago. It's always been one of my special places."

So, she was still on Garrity property? She hadn't even left their land. He stroked a finger down her cheek, not stopping until it tucked under her chin. He further lifted her face. Angling his head down, he hesitated only a moment, then he brushed his lips to hers. As always, the touch of his mouth was electric. Warm and firm, it pressured hers, although it didn't have to. She opened for him, wanting the kiss more than anything. Except, maybe, for the rest of him, which she wanted to feel hard and hot inside her again, the way it felt they were meant to be. "What were you thinking about?"

"You."

It was too good to be true. Magical. Her heart burst with wonder. "I didn't want to reverse the spell, and I didn't want to hurt you, but it just didn't seem right..."

"I thought you didn't want me to care for you—"

"No," she whispered. "It wasn't that."

He didn't speak immediately, and she became aware that their surroundings were otherworldly. Almost surreal. Far from the city, she could hear waves crashing, the rough sea propelled by forces of nature that even centuries of scientists couldn't understand. Sheets of rain fell around them like a waterfall, and she'd never felt so alone with another person, as if they were the only two people left in the world.

"I was thinking about how much I didn't want you to leave," he murmured.

Her breath caught. "But I cast a spell on your brother. Then reversed it, making you think that..."

"But you do care about me. You were just trying to make sure all this is real."

"All this?"

"Us."

"Is it?"

His amber eyes glazed with lust. Their skin was no longer cool from the weather, but heated from within. The aching tips of her breasts were peaking with longing; wet and cold from her shirt, they were warmed by the inferno of his chest, and suddenly, Signe simply couldn't stand it any longer. Whatever their superficial differences, the kind of heat they shared would ensure they could work things out.

Urgently, she glided a finger upward, opening the buttons of her blouse, not stopping until the front catch of her bra was released and her breasts were bare against his chest. She gasped, her jaw slackening at the contact, her eyes nearly shutting, a pang of need causing her to arch against his male heat, grinding hungrily.

"Why wouldn't I forgive you?" he murmured rhetorically, swooping down and kissing her, plundering her mouth with his own, their tongues meshing. "I missed you so much. I missed this." His voice broke as he slid his flattened palms down the sides of her drenched skirt. Grasping the hem, he forced the fabric upward on her thighs until he was touching her panties, pulling them down. "Needed this."

"Me, too," she managed to say raspily, her head giddy over the uncanny electricity coursing between them. "I don't know if it's lingering witchcraft," she whispered in anticipation, thinking her girlfriends were never going to believe a word of this, "or maybe because I just handled the statue of Eros. Or maybe just our chemistry…"

"Whatever it is," he returned as her fingers hooked into the waistband of his trunks, "the old saying holds."

She was panting too hard to talk. The long, gorgeous length of him was free now, and she was ready for him. "The saying?"

"Never look a gift horse in the mouth."

His lips met hers then. The moistened tip of his erection probed her folds, seeking her without the guidance of his hands, moving where nature intended. She opened for him, just as instinctively, crying as he lifted her, her legs circling his waist, her hands curling on his shoulders, bracing for sex that she knew would be as stormy as the winds. "You really don't care that this started when I cast a spell?"

He shook his head solemnly, even though he was at her opening, poised to enter her. "However it started, I'm liking how it's turning out," he said, his voice raspy. "Besides, I don't really believe in magic, Signe."

Looking into her eyes, how could he deny it? Excitement hitched, and she felt bubbly with it. "Really?"

"Not that kind of magic."

"What kind, then?"

"This kind." Just as he pushed deep inside, thunder sounded. Lightning brightened the sky, propelling him deeper, dazzling her with their own private electrical show, and as he buried himself, she realized he was right. However this began, she already knew how it would end. She knew it by the way he claimed her mouth once more, his searing lips covering hers for another sweet, hot, probing kiss that could only mean one word for them both: *forever.*

HARLEQUIN®

Temptation.

When the spirits are willing...
Anything can happen!

Welcome to the Inn at Maiden Falls, Colorado. Once a
brothel in the 1800s, the inn is now a successful honeymoon
resort. Only, little does anybody guess that all that marital
bliss comes with a little supernatural persuasion....

Don't miss this fantastic new miniseries. Watch for:

#977 SWEET TALKIN' GUY by Colleen Collins
June 2004

#981 CAN'T BUY ME LOVE by Heather MacAllister
July 2004

#985 IT'S IN HIS KISS by Julie Kistler
August 2004

THE SPIRITS
ARE WILLING

Available wherever Harlequin books are sold.

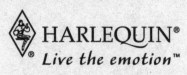

HARLEQUIN®
Live the emotion™

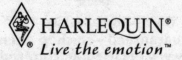

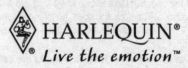

HARLEQUIN®

Temptation.

New York Times bestselling author

VICKI LEWIS THOMPSON

**celebrates Temptation's 20th anniversary—
and her own—in:**

#980

OLD ENOUGH TO KNOW BETTER

When twenty-year-old PR exec Kasey Braddock accepts
her co-workers' dare to hit on the gorgeous new landscaper,
she's excited. Finally, here's her chance to prove to her
friends—and herself—that she's woman enough to entice
a man and leave him drooling. After all, she's old enough
to know what she wants—and she wants Sam Ashton.
Luckily, he's not complaining....

Available in June wherever Harlequin books are sold.